SHADOW SURVIVOR

THE SHADOW AGENCY
BOOK 5

CHRISTY BARRITT

River Heights

CHAPTER
ONE

HEIDI MYERS BALANCED a bag of groceries on her hip as she unlocked the door to her townhouse. As the wind swept inside behind her, bringing with it an autumn chill and a smattering of rain, she quickly shoved the door closed.

Thunder shook the house as she did.

That was some storm raging out there. The wind howled, and rain poured from the sky like a never-ending waterfall.

But now, Heidi was back home, where she could dry off, warm up, and make herself a nice dinner.

She let her purse slide off her shoulder to the floor, reached for the light switch beside her, and flipped it.

Nothing happened.

She frowned.

Had the storm somehow knocked out the electricity?

That would just be her luck. She'd find her way to the kitchen and put her groceries down. Then she'd figure out the power situation.

However, she had really been looking forward to some chicken alfredo tonight. An electrical outage might thwart her plans.

She started through her living room when the hair on her neck rose.

Something in the air felt different. But what? Was it just the storm?

Or . . . what if the power wasn't out because of the storm?

Cold fear spread through her.

Now that she thought about it, the streetlight was on outside. And she'd seen her neighbor's lights on, had seen them seated at the dinner table together. But with her curtains closed, no light shone inside to guide her steps other than a dull gray from the transom over her front door.

Her muscles tensed as her adrenaline kicked in.

Maybe she was overthinking this. That was probably it. Considering what she did for a living, she often felt on edge.

Things had been even more stressful lately. That was why she'd been looking forward to tonight so much. She desperately wanted the chance to relax and unwind. To forget about her boss's demands.

More thunder shook the house.

She quickened her steps and made it to the kitchen. She flipped the light switch there.

Still nothing.

Before she set the paper bag on the counter, a noise caught her ear.

Her refrigerator was still humming, she realized.

Her gaze went to the stove.

Blue illuminated numbers stared back at her from the clock there.

She still had electricity. So why didn't her lights work?

Shivers raced up her spine.

Then movement sounded in the distance.

The barely perceptible sound of footsteps crossing the sage-colored shag rug in her living room hit her.

The paper bag fell from her hands. Oranges rolled across the floor. Eggs cracked. Milk began to glug out through a crack in the plastic jug.

"Who's there?" Her voice trembled as she gripped the kitchen counter.

Did she have time to step back and grab a knife from the butcher block across the kitchen? She didn't think so.

"We need to talk," a deep voice said.

Her heart beat double time. "Who are you?"

She blinked, praying her eyes would adjust to the darkness.

But they didn't.

All she knew was that the voice sounded vaguely familiar.

Her mind raced as she tried to put together where she'd heard it before.

Then the truth hit her.

She *did* know that voice.

But her comfort only lasted a moment before terror filled her.

The man in her home was a cold-blooded, trained assassin.

A cold-blooded, trained assassin who'd recently gone rogue.

———

Stephen Garner rose from his seat in Heidi's house.

He'd been waiting twenty minutes for her to return home.

He hated to do things this way, but he had no other choice. He couldn't be seen talking to her. He couldn't be seen period.

No one could know about this conversation.

Which was why the first thing he'd done when he

arrived was to check her place and make sure it wasn't bugged.

He'd found one camera and two listening devices. He'd destroyed them all.

Finding those things hadn't surprised him. When Heidi had accepted her current job, she'd had no idea what she was getting herself into. That was why he'd secretly been trying to watch out for her over the past few years.

He stepped closer to her shadowed figure, hating the fact he'd scared her so badly. "I just want to talk."

"Talk about what?" Her voice trembled.

"About your job."

"I . . . I can't talk about my job. Please. You're going to get me in trouble."

Even though it was dark, he sensed her anxiety. Saw the outline of movement as Heidi rubbed her hand across her chest as if to loosen the muscles.

He'd seen her do it before when she was nervous.

He'd noticed other things about her also. How she drank too much coffee. How that same coffee led her to use breath mints throughout the day. How she loved inspirational quotes and had them hung around her desk.

His intention hadn't been to scare her like this. If he had any better option, he would have taken it.

"I don't want to get you in trouble," he assured

her. "That's why I made sure no one knows I'm here. So we could have this conversation in private."

She paused. Stopped rubbing her chest. Drew in a deep breath. Then said, "You're Stephen. Stephen Garner. Thirty-four years old. The guy who's always picked for the hardest assignments since you have both the brawn and the brains, which can be an unusual combination. Except when it comes to the people you work with. You're all exceptional. You're the best of the best."

In other circumstances, he might be flattered. Right now, he was definitely impressed.

He'd known it was a possibility Heidi would recognize his voice. But she'd done so quickly. She'd remembered all the other details faster than he'd thought she would as well.

"Since those formalities are out of the way, then I guess I can get down to business," he said. "I need to find Rafferty."

"Rafferty? I don't know where he is."

Stephen stepped closer. He sensed Heidi's nerves starting to rear up like a hot wire. He could practically hear her heart racing as if someone had pushed the fast-forward button.

"What do you mean you don't know where he is?" Stephen asked. "You're his righthand man. Or woman."

"I mean what I said," Heidi told him. "I have no idea where he might be right now."

He took another step closer. "He's your boss. How can you not know his whereabouts? His home address?"

"We mostly talk on the phone and only meet a few times a year." Her voice trembled. "He's very private."

"You mean you've worked for him for four years, and in all that time, you've never seen his address on any paperwork? Never been to a dinner at his place?"

"Have you? You worked for him for a long time. Longer than I have. Do you know where he lives? Have you been to his house?"

"Touché." She had an excellent point.

But this woman was Stephen's best chance of figuring out how to locate this man. Rafferty had gone dark over the past couple of weeks. He hadn't been seen or heard from.

Thunder cracked overhead, and Heidi jumped.

He studied her, unconvinced she was telling the entire truth. She had access to information others in the company didn't.

"You guys are trained security agents," Heidi said. "If you wanted to find him, why didn't you track him? Follow him home? Do something other than hassling me?"

"He's very careful to cover his tracks."

"Then I don't know why you think I'd know."

He took another step closer.

Heidi drew in a sharp breath, and her eyes widened as she took a step back, fear filling her gaze. "Please . . . don't hurt me."

His brow furrowed. "Why would I hurt you?"

"You're here. In my house. You did something to my lights. Now you're making demands. Please . . . I don't want to die."

CHAPTER
TWO

STEPHEN'S FACE flashed in Heidi's mind.

She'd seen him and talked to him plenty of times before. The man was tall and burly with short, dark hair and a matching beard and mustache. His eyes were what always got to her. They were dark and intelligent, showing a sharp, observant man who let very few details get past him.

She trembled even thinking about what this man was capable of.

All Stephen had to do was to take a couple more steps, and she'd be within his reach. He had the capacity and strength to break someone's neck in two seconds flat.

But she also knew he could be friendly. Warm even. They'd had good banter at times at the office when she'd met the team there to go over assignments with them. He'd joked with her about her coffee addiction. About her obsession with breath mints. Once he'd even brought her coffee and a bag of her favorite wintergreen Lifesavers.

The juxtaposition had fascinated her and made her want to dig deeper into the man's background and psyche. But she hadn't—of course. There were professional boundaries in place.

Which Stephen was in her house now? The scary man who could kill her? Or the kind man who'd brought her coffee?

He lowered his voice as he said, "I'm not here to harm you, Heidi."

She still gripped the counter. When lightning flashed through the transom, she saw Stephen's outline.

His broad figure and bulky muscles were intimidating, to say the least.

She remembered his words. *I'm not here to harm you, Heidi.* He'd sounded so sincere.

But was he?

He waited for her response.

She licked her lips before saying, "If you don't intend to hurt me, then why are you here? Why did you break in like this?"

"It's like I said. So we could talk. Privately.

Without Rafferty finding out. Besides, if I'd wanted to hurt you—"

"You would have by now?" Heidi finished for him as she let his words settle.

They made sense. Rafferty was the type who always had people watching. For that reason, Heidi could never fully let down her guard.

"How do you know Rafferty doesn't know?" It was a question she often asked herself. It seemed like nothing she did was private. Her boss seemed to have eyes everywhere.

"I cleared two bugs and one camera from your home. I watched to make sure I wasn't followed, and I entered your house through the back—after parking four blocks away and using a motorcycle I borrowed from a friend."

Her eyebrows shot up. He really had thought of everything.

Then part of what he said hit her.

"You found bugs in my house?" she whispered. "A camera?"

"That's right. You're too much of an asset for Rafferty to simply let you live your life. He monitors everything you say and do. But I have a feeling you already suspected that."

Heidi continued to grip the counter, her mind racing.

Yes, she'd suspected some of those things before. But hearing Stephen's confirmation . . . it sent chills through her.

"Where exactly was this camera?" The thought was disturbing on so many levels.

"In your living room."

In some ways, that was a relief, she supposed. But it was still an invasion of her privacy at the highest level.

Had Rafferty left those to keep an eye on her? Or someone else? Maybe one of Blackstone's enemies?

Her throat tightened as she tried to figure out her next move. "So you just want to talk?"

"That's right."

"Do we need to talk in the darkness like this?"

"I can turn the lights back on—as long as you promise not to do anything foolish in the meantime."

"Define foolish."

"Calling the police or Rafferty would only end up getting us both in trouble." He paused and lowered his voice. "I promise I'm not here to hurt you, Heidi. You're the only person I could think of who could help."

"Help with what?"

"Help bring James Rafferty down."

She swallowed hard. Bring her boss down?

The idea might seem absurd. However, after

hearing about a few of his latest assignments, she was now curious.

She'd always wondered if the man was up to no good. Maybe this was her chance to find out more about who she was really working for.

However, she wasn't sure she could handle the truth.

———

Stephen prayed his words were getting through to Heidi. That she would help him instead of turning on him.

Right now, everything depended on her decision.

He wished he could see her face. That he could read her mind, for that matter.

He couldn't do those things, but he could use his other abilities. His power of observation had been highly tuned.

He could hear Heidi's quick breathing, which let him know she was still nervous.

He could feel the stillness in the room, as if she were frozen, trying to make a decision.

He could hear her swallow as she was about to speak.

Finally, she sighed and crossed her arms. "Okay. I don't know what I can do for you, but we can talk."

He hoped her words were sincere. "Perfect."

He walked into the living room. He reached for the beige lamp on an end table, snaked his hand through the shade, and screwed in the bulb. Its glow instantly filled the room.

As he turned, he caught a glimpse of Heidi.

Of her heart-shaped face. Her light brown hair. Her thick, curly ringlets. Her petite frame.

He couldn't see the smattering of freckles across her nose and cheeks from across the room, but he knew they were there. He could easily picture her bright green eyes and straight teeth. He'd practically memorized all her features—not that his attraction to her mattered. He'd even flirted with her on occasion, but he knew those playful interactions would go nowhere.

His past prevented any future relationships. He was too broken.

However, he hated that he'd scared Heidi as he did. But he'd had no other choice.

Milk puddled on the tile floor at her feet. Two eggs were smattered, the yolks bleeding from them. Oranges had scattered from the bag as if desperate to make an escape.

Right now, it didn't matter. There would be time to pick those things up later.

"Do you want to sit down?" he suggested.

Heidi still looked uncertain. Her gaze showed she was calculating her response, weighing her options.

Finally, she nodded. "Okay."

Stephen watched as she stepped over the bag and headed to the couch. She sat tentatively as she stared at him.

He sat in the chair across from her, wishing he could put her more at ease.

He'd always liked Heidi. He'd enjoyed their conversations when they'd talked in the past. He'd even looked forward to seeing her at work. Her cheery face was always a welcome sight after their assignments.

Then he'd discovered the truth about his own background—and Rafferty's role in all of it.

Stephen left Blackstone, a top-secret security company, and teamed up with other men who were just like him—who were fighting to take down those who wanted too much power and control. People like Rafferty.

Rafferty was their current focus. They needed to find him. Interrogate him. Learn what he was up to.

Ever since Stephen had defected from the security group, he felt certain he'd been targeted. He'd found bugs in his own apartment. Had sensed someone following him. Had seen his bank account unexplainably drained.

That meant he needed to be a shadow. Each of his moves had to be planned and executed very carefully.

"What do you want to know?" Heidi rubbed her hands across her dark-wash blue jeans, clearly nervous.

"Everything. I need to know everything you know—and maybe more."

She blinked as if overwhelmed and shook her head. "You are going to have to be a little more specific. I'm only his executive assistant. It's not like he gives me open access to all the information about the company."

Before Stephen could say anything else, a footstep sounded outside.

Most people probably wouldn't have heard it. But his instincts had been fine-tuned through years of training and experience.

Heidi sat up straighter. "What is it?"

He rose. "Are you expecting anyone?"

"No. I was just going to make dinner for myself. No one else."

He was afraid of that. "Someone's here. He's going to be at your door in about ten seconds."

"He?"

"The footsteps are heavy. It's a man."

Heidi's eyebrows flicked up as if she were impressed.

Stephen locked his gaze with hers. "You can't tell anybody I'm here. Do you understand?"

"Y—yeah . . . yes," she stuttered. "Of course."

He quickly considered his options. He could stand behind the door, but if the man came inside, he'd be spotted. He didn't want things to turn volatile.

The coat closet, he decided. That was where he could hide.

He darted toward it, remaining light on his feet. Before he slipped inside, he turned toward Heidi and whispered, "If you tell this person I'm here, there will be consequences."

Were his words a threat? Yes, he supposed in some ways they were. But he didn't plan on hurting Heidi.

Yet there *would* be consequences.

It would be to both of their detriments if he was discovered.

He stared at Heidi, waiting for her response.

Finally, she nodded. "I'll handle it."

Stephen slipped into the closet, closed the door, and prayed for the best.

CHAPTER
THREE

THIS COULD BE Heidi's chance to get away from Stephen. The person on the other side of the door could be the key to her safety—and an answer to prayer.

Part of her wanted to trust Stephen. She'd been fascinated with the man for years now.

But also afraid.

Not because he'd ever done anything to make her feel fearful toward him. But because she knew what he was capable of. She'd seen his intimidating stance and thick muscles. They were enough to frighten anybody.

But his eyes . . . they'd told a different story. They were compassionate and wise.

He was unlike most of Rafferty's guys, and for that reason, she'd always been drawn to him.

A moment later, just as Stephen had predicted, a knock sounded at the door.

Heidi ran a hand through her hair, down her black oversized cardigan, and then across her blue jeans. Then she drew in a deep breath and stepped closer.

The closet was right behind the front door. If Stephen really were the ogre she feared he might be, he could easily jump out and stop her from doing anything he considered foolish. But she had a feeling he wanted to stay below the radar.

"Heidi?" a deep voice called.

Right away, she knew who was here. But the realization didn't bring her any comfort.

"Open up," the man outside called. "I know you're in there."

She took one more glance at the closet door and contemplated her actions.

Then, with a certain sense of resignation, she pulled open her front door.

Beau Glasser stood outside, lightning flashing behind him.

Another Blackstone team member.

Stephen's former colleague.

The man was imposing but in a different way than Stephen.

Some of the guys seemed like mostly muscle.

Smart, yes. But they simply did what they were told and never asked questions. Never checked their conscience.

Beau was one of those guys . . .

He was tall and strong with hair so short he almost looked bald. His jaw was always flexing as if he constantly gritted his teeth, and his hands were usually fisted. He reminded her of a living, breathing, ticking time bomb.

"Beau . . . what are you doing here?" she asked.

Heidi had said the man's name aloud for Stephen's benefit—although he'd probably recognized the voice.

"Rafferty told me to check on you," Beau stated, his voice gruff and cold.

"I'm fine." She rubbed a hand over her chest. "Why would he be concerned?"

"Someone might be targeting Blackstone. We need to make sure all our team members are secure."

Her throat burned as the seriousness of the situation hit her. "I appreciate the concern, but I'm fine."

"You only think you're fine."

She rubbed her arms. "Now you're scaring me. Obviously, there's more to this story than you're telling me. Is someone specifically threatening me?"

"Not really. We just need to be careful. I'm going

to station myself outside your house tonight just to make sure you're safe. Rafferty's orders."

"Okay then. That seems like overkill, but if you insist." Heidi could only assume Stephen would figure out a way to get out of her house without being seen. He'd gotten inside that way.

Did Beau suspect Stephen was here? Was that what all this was about?

When Beau stepped back, relief tried to flood her. But before Heidi allowed the emotion to wash over her, Beau's eyes drifted behind her.

She tensed. He'd seen the groceries on the floor, hadn't he?

Now his suspicions were raised.

Heidi would have to think of something. Fast.

————

"What happened there?" Stephen heard his former colleague mutter.

He'd recognized Beau's voice right away.

The man wasn't Stephen's favorite person. He was too mindless. Too reactive. Didn't have enough of a conscience.

For some reason, Beau had shown up here at Heidi's. Had Rafferty sent him knowing that Stephen was here?

He couldn't be sure.

"What happened to your groceries?" Beau clarified.

"Oh, those?" Heidi let out a nervous laugh. "That's nothing. I was too lazy to turn on my light when I walked in. Thought I knew this place like the back of my hand. Then I missed the countertop."

"I saw you walk inside ten minutes ago. I'm surprised you haven't cleaned that up yet."

Stephen's heart beat harder. He'd hoped Beau had overlooked the timing, but Stephen should have known better. The man had been trained to be observant.

What would Heidi say?

"Well, if you must know, part of the reason I dropped the groceries is because I was in a rush to go to the bathroom. Female issues, and trust me, you don't want to know details. Anyway, I'd just come out of the bathroom and was about to clean up the mess when you knocked on the door. I didn't realize I would be interrogated about it, or I would've picked everything up right away."

Stephen's eyebrows rose. He was impressed. Heidi had done a good job coming up with that story on the fly.

He'd always known she was smart. Rafferty had pulled her away from a job as an administrator at a

Fortune 500 company and got her to come work for him. Stephen could only imagine the job offer had to be pretty enticing for her to say yes.

His throat clenched. He knew there was actually more to the story than that.

Heidi had taken the job out of necessity after her mom was in a terrible car accident that left her a quadriplegic and unable to care for herself. Heidi had taken care of her for four years until her mom passed away last year.

Stephen had done his research and had been surprised at the details he'd found out about Heidi's life.

Those details made him want to know more.

"I need to check out your place," Beau said. "Just to be safe."

"That won't be necessary—"

Stephen knew Beau would check out her townhouse despite Heidi's objections. What would Stephen do when Beau reached the closet?

His heart pounded as he thought of the implications.

Footsteps sounded. Beau had walked away, avoiding the closet—for now.

"I didn't invite you in," Heidi murmured. "This feels intrusive."

"Not my problem," Beau told her.

Thunder cracked outside.

As they moved farther away, Stephen could no longer make out what they were saying. Had Heidi and Beau gone upstairs? If so, this could be Stephen's chance to get out of here.

But he would have to move quickly or this could turn ugly.

Very ugly.

CHAPTER
FOUR

"AS YOU CAN SEE, everything is fine." Heidi rushed to keep in step with Beau as he charged into her house like he owned the place. "I'm not even sure what you're looking for. Do you think I'm hiding something here?"

"I need to make sure there are no safety concerns." He went into the kitchen and opened a few cabinets, as well as the door to her walk-in pantry.

"Safety concerns . . . in my cabinets?" Her confusion turned into irritation.

He continued to storm the house, checking every crevice and behind every curtain.

Then another thought hit her. Stephen had said he found a couple of bugs as well as a camera in the house. Had Rafferty sent Beau here when those things went offline?

Maybe.

Because Rafferty *had* to be the one who had those planted here. He was the only one who made sense. She might try to convince herself otherwise, but when it came to Rafferty . . . the shoe fit.

Beau headed upstairs toward her bedroom, still acting as if he were on a war path.

She scrambled to keep up with him but managed to remain on his heels. "Like I said, everything is fine."

Beau grunted and headed toward her bedroom.

Typical Beau. The company currently employed twelve security operatives, many of them just like Beau. Others had come and gone over the years, some rougher than others. All of them had an air of mystery about them, however.

He searched her room, her bathroom, and her two spare bedrooms.

Then he headed downstairs again, unable to be deterred.

"Just one more place to check, and I'll be out of your hair." Beau started toward the coat closet.

The closet hiding Stephen.

Panic filled her. Heidi had to stop Beau before he opened that door. But how?

Her thoughts raced as she glanced around.

She had to do something.

On second thought, maybe Stephen being discovered was the best thing.

He had ambushed her in her own home, after all.

But he hadn't hurt her. She wanted to believe she could trust the dangerous but fascinating man.

She didn't have much time to decide who to trust.

She had to follow her gut instinct.

Stephen, she decided. She trusted Stephen.

Just as Beau reached the door, she screamed.

He spun around. "What in tarnation is wrong, woman?"

"A mouse!" Her hands covered her heart. "It just ran across the floor. Get it!"

He scowled at her, looking annoyed.

Then he opened the door anyway.

So much for that idea.

I'm so sorry, Stephen. But a mouse was the best I could come up with.

Heidi braced herself for whatever would happen next.

————

Stephen shifted uncomfortably as he stood stiffly in the small pantry.

This was the only place he'd been able to stash himself before Heidi and Beau came back downstairs.

He had to be careful not to move and accidentally knock a can of beans or a box of pasta off the shelf behind him.

That would be a dead giveaway to his presence—something he couldn't risk.

He continued to listen to the conversation in the living room.

"I think the mouse went in there! It was a big one. Maybe a rat." Panic filled Heidi's voice.

"Overreact much?"

"Rude much?"

A smile tugged at Stephen's lips. At least Heidi had given it right back to Beau.

She'd had to be tough when working with the Blackstone operatives.

She'd tried her best to stop Beau from opening the door to the closet where Stephen had been hiding.

Good. That probably meant she trusted him—at least somewhat. That she was on his side and not Beau's.

That was a good start, but they still had a long way to go.

"I'll be outside," Beau said. "Call me if you need anything. Got it?"

"If you insist," Heidi said. "I would have put together a dossier on this assignment if Rafferty had given me a heads up."

"You should just be happy that I'm here."

Stephen heard a door open and a grunt. "I don't see any rats. You sure you weren't seeing things?"

"I . . . uh, well . . . I guess I was."

Beau grunted again. "I'm going to put a camera on your back door also so I can monitor that side of the house."

A camera on the back door? Great. That would make it even more complicated for Stephen to get out of here. But he'd figure out something.

He drew in another deep breath as he reminded himself to remain frozen.

"Will you need to come inside to do that?" Heidi asked.

"No, I want you to lock up as soon as I leave. I can do everything I need from outside."

"Perfect, because I need to clean up my groceries and make dinner." She paused. "You really think I'm in danger?"

"Yep." Beau's answer was succinct, and he offered no other details.

Stephen waited as he heard the door close. The lock click in place. Heard Heidi pace down the hallway. Another door being locked.

Then footsteps padded back toward the kitchen.

"Stephen?" The words came out at a harsh whisper. "Where are you?"

He nudged open the pantry door, thankful the space had been sizable enough to accommodate his large frame.

As soon as Heidi spotted him, her expression softened. "I thought for sure you were going to be discovered."

"Thankfully, you guys went upstairs and afforded me the opportunity to find another hiding spot."

She rubbed a hand over her chest, her eyes closed. "I'm glad. I didn't know how I would explain having you in my closet."

"You wouldn't have had to explain. Beau would've realized what was going on and tried to kill me." His eyebrows flicked upward in a matter-of-fact manner.

She opened her eyes, and they widened until they were as big as a full moon on a cloudless night. "Look, I'm so sorry to hear about everything that's happened. But I don't know how much I can help you."

He shushed her, motioning for her to keep her voice down. They couldn't afford for Beau to hear them talking.

Stephen walked into the living room and turned

on the TV. As a news story filled the air, he knew the noise would conceal part of their conversation.

It was right on time too. A thump sounded at the back door—Beau installing that new camera.

His presence made this situation even trickier.

"What do we do now?" Heidi stared up at him, studying his gaze as if hoping he might have some answers.

Stephen hadn't expected Beau to show up. He had to recalculate.

"I'm going to be stuck here," he said. "Since your townhouse is sandwiched between two others, I can only get out the front and back doors—neither of which will work right now."

"It sounds like we're going to be together for a while." Heidi tilted her head. "So how about you help me clean up and start dinner because I'm starving."

Something about her words caused a smile to tug at his lips.

Her plan almost sounded too normal. But normal was what Stephen had been craving lately, so he wouldn't argue.

It had been a long time since he'd experienced normal. Since his adoptive parents had died, he supposed. He'd been eleven at the time, and every-thing had been different since then. From being shuffled to various homes to finding his own way to work out his grief—through cage fighting.

Then he'd been plucked out of that life and into an equally tough position with Project Elevate.

Still, he had to remain on guard. This situation could turn even more violent at any moment.

He didn't trust Beau. The man was too fond of whispered conversations. He had the tendency to disappear at the worst times. Once, he'd even left Stephen in the middle of a mission. Had claimed it was a misunderstanding. Stephen had almost been killed.

He didn't like having the man outside. Didn't know exactly what his former colleague was up to.

For that reason, Stephen would have to plan his next moves very carefully.

CHAPTER
FIVE

HEIDI'S STOMACH GRUMBLED, offering a temporary distraction from her otherwise heavy thoughts.

While Stephen grabbed a chair and tightened the kitchen light until illumination filled the space, she quickly picked up the bag of groceries she'd purchased and salvaged what she could. As she sorted through the pasta and veggies still in the paper bag, Stephen screwed in another loose light-bulb. Then he grabbed the wayward oranges and placed them on the table. He got some paper towels and began to clean up the milk and eggs on the floor.

"Do you like chicken alfredo?" She held up a package of chicken.

He placed a finger over his lips, reminding her to keep her voice low. "Yes, I do."

"You think Beau can hear us talking?" she whispered loudly.

"I wouldn't put anything past him." Stephen stepped farther into the kitchen. "What can I help with?"

"You can make the salad while I start the noodles."

"I can handle that."

She knew exactly what Stephen could handle—and it was a lot.

She didn't know much about the men who worked for Blackstone. She knew they'd been part of some type of special operations for the military. Their missions may have even been off-the-books.

From what she understood, Rafferty had been their leader. When he'd left his station with the military, he'd taken his guys with him.

He'd started Blackstone, his own security firm. His company had taken on tough jobs—private jobs —often for high-profile clients.

Her duties included arranging transportation and housing for these assignments. She handled the details while Rafferty made the decisions.

As the water began to boil, Heidi poured some penne noodles into the bubbling liquid. While they cooked, she would heat up the alfredo sauce.

On some occasions, she might try to make the

sauce herself. But not today. There was so much the two of them needed to talk about. Yet the moment felt surprisingly casual.

Either way, she was stuck with Stephen for the foreseeable future.

She pulled out the raw chicken and began to slice it. "So what are you trying to find out? I need more information here."

He grabbed a container of prewashed romaine lettuce from the fridge and set it on a wooden cutting board. "I need to track down Rafferty, and you're the only one who can help me do that."

"What makes you think I can help you?" They'd been over this already. "I'm sorry to disappoint you, but I don't know where he is."

"Even if you don't know where he is, you most likely have information that could lead us to his whereabouts." He began chopping the lettuce into small pieces.

"I don't know why you think I have that information. I coordinate assignments. I hook you guys up with the equipment you need. With accommodations. Transportation. But Rafferty is only my boss."

"Do you send him a paycheck?"

She added some olive oil to her frying pan. "No, he pays himself directly."

"Do you have a record of the payroll trans-actions?"

"I don't do the bookkeeping," she said. "Rafferty takes care of that himself, and I simply process the direct deposits on payday."

He placed the lettuce into a wooden bowl that Heidi pulled out. "You don't need to check to make sure he has money in any accounts?"

"No, Rafferty assured me that there would always be money. I just need approval for anything over five thousand dollars."

Stephen's jaw twitched as he grabbed a tomato from a wire basket on the counter. "Then maybe we can somehow pinpoint his location based on your correspondence."

She added the chicken to the pan and listened to it sizzle. "You can try, but I think we both know that's not going to work. He has all the proper precautions in place."

Stephen frowned as he turned on the water and rinsed the tomato. "That's not what I want to hear."

"See?" As the chicken continued to sizzle in the pan, she glanced up at him. "I told you I wouldn't be much help. I'm sorry you've gone through all this trouble for nothing."

Yet the other part of her wasn't sorry. She didn't need any more complications in her life. She liked to keep things simple. One way she could do that was by not entertaining this conversation any longer than necessary.

This job had seemed like a godsend when she'd been hired. The position had allowed her to work mostly from home so she could take care of her mom. A few times a week, she would go to an office located in a standalone building outside Atlanta. That was where she would meet the teams before they went out on their assignments. She would give them a rundown, hand them supplies, and wish them well.

Rafferty had simply given Heidi the assignments and trusted her to handle the details.

But if Heidi were honest with herself, she'd admit she'd wondered over the past several months if there wasn't more going on in this organization than met the eye.

Had she helped empower Rafferty's men to do terrible things?

She prayed that wasn't the case.

———

Stephen watched Heidi's face as they sat across the dining room table from each other.

She wasn't naive. He knew that. But she also didn't have a great poker face. When she considered lying, her lips turned down in a frown for a split second. When she was nervous, she rubbed her chest.

For those reasons, he thought Heidi really was telling the truth.

She didn't know where Rafferty lived. Everything she'd told him about the way Rafferty did business had rung true.

The man had covered all his bases.

She sprinkled some grated parmesan onto her pasta and then handed the bowl to Stephen. "I don't understand what's going on. You obviously don't trust Rafferty. But you're making this situation seem like life or death."

"It *is* life or death." He lifted a spoon full of cheese over his plate. "My friends and I had devices implanted near our hearts, without our knowledge or permission. Rafferty controlled the devices and used them to stop our hearts—to try and kill us."

Heidi gasped as his words hit her. "That can't be possible."

He locked gazes with her. "Not only is it possible, but it also really happened. One man is still on life-support in the hospital. He's been there for the past ten days."

She rubbed her neck. "That's terrible. I've always known Rafferty was former military and that the team under him did some sketchy assignments. But I never imagined it was anything like that."

Stephen tilted his head. "All these assignments we've done, and you never thought that someone could get hurt in the process?"

Her cheeks reddened as she gripped her fork, about to stab her pasta. "Maybe sometimes I just want to ignore things. Convince myself that the ends justify the means. I don't know enough details to make any judgments. Besides, I feel like it isn't my business."

He could respect that. In this line of work, boundaries were essential.

"Rafferty is a dangerous man," Stephen continued, determined to drive home his point. "We don't know what he's planning next. However, we are certain he's up to no good. That's why we have to bring him down."

"Who is *we*?"

"Some other men who were in his program but defected along with me."

Compassion flooded her gaze. "I wish I could help you. I really do. But I think you've come to the wrong person. I have no idea how to locate Rafferty."

"When was the last time you spoke?"

Before she could respond, Heidi's phone rang on the table beside her.

She glanced at it, and her face went pale.

Her gaze darted to meet Stephen's. "Speak of the devil . . . it's Rafferty. He's calling me right now."

Stephen sucked in a breath before muttering, "Perfect. Answer and put it on speaker. Let's hear what he has to say."

CHAPTER
SIX

STEPHEN WAITED for Heidi to touch the phone.

Heidi's gaze flittered about as if she were uncertain if answering was wise.

"I won't indicate I'm here," he assured her. "I promise. But I *am* going to try to trace the call."

He pulled a device from his pocket, one his colleague had given him before Stephen had come here. He quickly plugged it into Heidi's phone and watched a screen appear on his device.

Finally, she drew in a deep breath and hit the Talk button.

"Good evening," Heidi started. "I wasn't expecting to hear from—"

"Heidi, we have a new job that just came in." Rafferty's gruff voice barked across the line. "I need you to take care of the details for me."

She glanced at Stephen. He nodded to let her know to keep going.

"Of course." Her voice sounded tense. "What do you need me to do?"

"I'll send you all the information about who I'd like assigned and what they'll need. I need you to work on it ASAP. I know it's last minute, but it's important."

"Got it. One more question." Heidi played with the pasta on her plate instead of eating it. Her appetite was clearly disappearing. "Beau is stationed outside my house. I don't understand what's going on. Why is he here?"

"The company has had some threats made against us. My guys can defend themselves. You can't."

Her gaze fluttered to Stephen's again. "You're making me nervous."

Stephen twirled his finger in the air, indicating she should keep talking. She was doing a good job with her subterfuge. He stored that fact away.

"You should be nervous," Rafferty told her. "That's why I want you to stay inside where it's safe. At least until this passes."

"Who's threatening you?" she asked. "Is it someone I should be aware of? Someone I should keep my eyes open for?"

"I'm not a hundred percent sure. But I'd keep my eyes open for Stephen Garner."

She gasped. "Stephen?"

"He's gone rogue."

Stephen bit down, grinding his teeth. That man was trying to turn Heidi against him.

Classic Rafferty move.

Her hands began to tremble. "Why? What happened?"

"You don't need to worry about those details. I've gotta go. I'm sending you the info now. Take care of it for me."

Before Heidi could ask more questions, the line went dead.

————

Heidi's hands trembled as she finished the call. She felt Stephen's gaze burning into her and lifted her eyes to meet his, not sure what she would find.

She halfway expected him to be angry that she hadn't been able to keep Rafferty on the phone longer.

Instead, compassion lined his gaze. "Good job. I know that wasn't easy, but you kept your composure."

His compliment caused a surge of warmth to rush

through her—though she tried not to show it. Her life had been so solitary lately. In truth, she'd felt a little lost and a lot lonely.

Rafferty certainly didn't give out compliments. She'd kept her boundaries up with the guys in the office. Stephen had been the exception.

She'd always known there was something different about him.

"He said I should watch out for you," she stated. She prayed the wool wasn't being pulled over her eyes.

"He's just trying to turn you against me."

She stared at him another moment, hoping he was telling the truth. Still uncertain, she licked her lips. "Were you able to locate Rafferty?"

Stephen shook his head. "Unfortunately, no."

"If Rafferty really is guilty of doing the things you said, then he needs to be brought down. I feel for you and your situation. I do. But I really don't know what else I can do."

Stephen's gaze bore into hers. "He had bugs in your house. A camera. No matter what you think you might know about your boss, it's wrong. He's looking out for one person, and that person is himself. Everyone else is disposable to him."

Heidi's heart lurched into her throat at the words. She wanted to deny that he might be right. But how could she? If what Stephen was telling her was true, then Heidi had unwillingly been drawn into a dangerous game.

She swallowed hard. She needed to figure out exactly what to do.

She glanced at the barely touched food on her plate. "I need to disseminate the information Rafferty sent. If I take too long, he'll be suspicious."

"I agree. I need to see what he sends you."

She pushed her plate away, knowing that her plans for a peaceful dinner had gone up in smoke.

Instead, she grabbed her work laptop and typed in several things. Then she turned the screen toward Stephen.

"The dossier looks pretty standard," she told him. "It's for an extraction. No details on the time and place. He requested three of his guys."

"Who?"

She scanned the list. "Three new guys. He told me he'd hired some new people after Vintage and Nathan died and you left. I actually haven't met them yet."

"He didn't make you help with the onboarding process?"

She shook her head. "There some things he likes to do himself. He's a bit of a control freak, if you haven't noticed."

"I have," he muttered.

"Basically, Rafferty just listed what equipment would be needed and when. Nothing ground-breaking."

She let Stephen study it a moment, and she took several more bites of her pasta. But her appetite had disappeared.

She didn't want to be in the middle of this, but she was.

Should she quit this job and find another?

She had a feeling it wouldn't be that easy. She was in too deep. She knew too much.

Stephen looked up at her, and Heidi knew she was about to receive more news she wasn't prepared for.

"I hate to ask you to do this," he started. "But I need someone to be the inside man—or woman—for us."

Her eyes widened. "You want me to spy on Rafferty for you? If he found out I was doing that . . ."

The grim expression remained on Stephen's face. "I know. It would be bad, and if there were any other way, I would take it. Believe me, I would. But you're our only hope of finding the information we need. Rafferty is an island, and you're the only lifeboat that will get us to him."

Heidi didn't like the sound of that.

She contemplated her options. Rafferty wouldn't let her walk away. If she tried to quit, he would never let her leave. And if he found out she was acting as a spy? He'd be furious.

Either way, she was in a dangerous position.

Before she could decide, the sound of glass shattering filled the air.

Then a smoky scent filled her nostrils.

"Get down!" Stephen yelled before throwing himself over her.

CHAPTER
SEVEN

STEPHEN'S ADRENALINE pumped as he realized something was on fire.

Heidi trembled beneath him, her eyes wide with terror.

"Stay here!" He stood from where his body had covered hers on the floor.

Staying low, he darted toward the living room.

Flames consumed the area rug.

He grabbed a blanket from the back of the couch and began to smother the flames.

As he did, the truth hit him: Someone had thrown a Molotov cocktail through Heidi's front window.

The person responsible was probably long gone.

Why hadn't Beau stopped them? Where was Beau now?

Stephen stomped out the last of the flames.

The rug was ruined. The coffee table charred. He wasn't sure what the floor looked like underneath it. Clearly, the window would need to be replaced.

But all things considered, he was grateful no one had been hurt. This could have been so much worse.

He strode to the window and nudged the curtain aside.

Beau's car still sat across the street out front.

But he didn't see Beau anywhere—not running toward the house or after the perpetrator.

Something was wrong.

"Stephen?" Heidi's voice sounded shaky as she called to him from the dining room.

He turned his head toward her. "I need to check things out outside. You should be safe in here—for now. Just stay where you are, okay?"

"O . . . okay."

She didn't sound certain, and he couldn't blame her in this situation. There were too many unknowns.

Drawing his gun, he stepped out the front door.

He knew exposing himself was risky. Someone could be trying to draw him out, for all he knew. But he had to see what was going on, even if that meant coming out of hiding.

He glanced around, searching the darkness for any signs of the person who'd started the fire. A row of high-end townhouses identical to Heidi's stood across the street. Several cars were parked in driveways.

He saw no one.

Most likely, the perpetrator had sped away after throwing the bottle through Heidi's window. The person was probably long gone, not wanting to be seen.

He eased closer to Beau's black Ford Explorer.

Was his former colleague inside? If not, where was he? What was he doing right now?

Stephen crept closer, remaining cautious.

Finally, he got a glimpse inside the car. The windshield was shattered.

Beau sat behind the steering wheel. His head leaned against the seat, and his eyes remained closed.

A bad feeling brewed in Stephen's gut as he peered closer.

It was just as he feared—a bullet hole pierced Beau's forehead.

Stephen's heart sped several beats.

Then he heard the sirens in the distance. One of Heidi's neighbors must have heard something and called the police.

But Stephen didn't want the police to find him. Nor did he want to leave Heidi.

He had to make a quick decision on what he would do.

———

Heidi remained huddled against the wall in her dining room, her knees pulled to her chest. She'd only moved enough to grab a knife from the kitchen. She gripped it, praying she didn't have to use it.

What was going on out there?

Finally, she heard the door open and someone step into the house.

Was it Stephen? Beau? Or someone else entirely?

She had no idea.

When Stephen entered the room, relief washed through her.

Based on the quickness of his steps and the tight set of his shoulders, he knew something.

She set the knife on the floor and straightened. "What is it?"

"Beau is dead. One of your neighbors must have called the police. I hear sirens."

She gasped, and her hand flew over her mouth, unsure if she'd heard correctly. "What?"

He nodded. "I'm sorry, but it's true."

"But who . . . what . . . ?"

"I don't know." He lowered his voice. "I don't want to do this to you. I really don't. But I need to leave before the police arrive."

"You're going to leave?" Panic filled her. "Right now?"

He grasped her shoulders as his gaze locked on hers. "Whoever did this is long gone. You'll be okay, and I'll stay close. I just can't be on record right now as being here with you. It's too risky."

"But . . ." The thought of being alone right now terrified her. She hadn't realized until this moment how much comfort she found in Stephen's presence.

The sirens came closer and closer.

He leveled his gaze with her. "I promise you'll be okay."

Something about his tone reassured her. She took a deep breath and nodded. "You'd better get going."

"I'm going to slip out the back door and take that camera with me. I have to make sure my face isn't recorded. I'll be in touch."

Her thoughts continued to race. "How?"

"I have your number. I'm not going to leave you, I promise. I just need to step into the shadows for a while."

With those words, he disappeared out the back door just as the lights from a police car and a fire truck appeared out front.

CHAPTER
EIGHT

THE NEXT MORNING, Heidi was still shaken from the events of last night. What happened almost seemed surreal.

After Stephen left, the police and fire department had shown up. Heidi had explained that something had been thrown through her front window. Had told them she had security detail outside due to the nature of her job. She'd let the police discover that Beau was dead instead of telling them herself.

Then the cops had come inside to investigate. There had been questions. So many questions. Heidi had told them what she could while trying not to tell them too much.

She didn't want them to know all the details of her job. Rafferty wouldn't want that information exposed. So she told them she worked for Blackstone, and she gave them Rafferty's number so they could follow up. He could decide what he wanted the cops to know.

One of Heidi's neighbors had come over with some plywood and helped her to secure the broken window. She'd rolled up the rug that had caught on fire and had tossed it out the back near the trash can. She kept her coffee table, hoping she could salvage it with a fresh coat of paint.

None of this seemed real.

Now it was a new day.

But she was on edge as she fixed herself some oatmeal for breakfast. She'd gotten out of bed early. Showered. Dressed in some jeans and her favorite comfy sweatshirt.

She halfway expected danger to pop up again. Or for Stephen to be hiding in her house. Or for someone to throw something else through another window.

But none of those things had happened.

Not yet at least.

Just as she took the last sip of her coffee, her phone rang. She saw Rafferty's number and quickly answered.

He bypassed any greetings and jumped right into the heart of the conversation. "Well, that was a catastrophe last night. An utter catastrophe."

It almost sounded as if he were blaming her, though she had nothing to do with what happened. And would it have really hurt him to ask how she was doing after the traumatic events?

She'd tried to call him last night and give him a report on what had happened. He hadn't answered, which wasn't totally unusual for him. But it was still frustrating.

Her resolve hardened. "I need to know what's going on."

She thought Stephen would be proud of her for her direct approach to getting information.

Though if she truly did get information, she wasn't sure if she'd share it with him or not. She thought she could trust him. But in this line of work, one had to be very careful about whom they trusted. Putting her faith in the wrong person could get her killed.

"I can't tell you what's going on." Rafferty's voice remained steely. "Besides, it's better if you don't know."

The muscles across Heidi's chest tightened, and she ran her hand over them. "You have to tell me something. I don't know how much longer I can live like this. My life is also in danger."

Those words were absolutely true. The past

twelve hours had painted her future in a different light. The situation felt impossible.

"Hopefully, it will be over soon. I have Donald working your detail. He's sitting outside your house right now."

She stood and walked to her door. She peered out the window atop it and saw another black SUV parked outside. "How do I know Donald isn't going to end up dead like Beau?"

"You don't. You let me worry about that."

"I don't want someone else killed on my account. And what about Beau? Did he have a family?"

"No, he didn't. We'll honor his legacy as soon as we're able."

As far as Heidi knew, none of the guys who worked for Rafferty had a family.

Really, it was strange. But she'd always told herself it wasn't her business. She constantly fell back on that logic. *The less she knew, the better. Keep things professional. Mind your own business.*

Those were all things she'd constantly told herself.

She could see now where that had been a mistake.

From the sounds of it, Rafferty wanted to keep her locked up inside indefinitely. The thought made her want to panic. She couldn't settle for that.

She leaned against her door, her heart pounding harder. "I don't want to hide out in my house."

"If you want to stay alive, then you don't have much choice."

Her jaw hardened. Rafferty wasn't making this easy. Then again, she hadn't expected him to.

"I'm not so sure it's safe being here," she countered. "Someone tried to burn my house down last night."

"What stopped them? Why didn't this person make sure he succeeded?"

She froze at his question. All she could hear was her heart as it pounded in her ears.

That was an excellent question.

Had it been because Stephen was inside?

For that matter, did Rafferty already know Stephen had been here? Was he testing her?

She had no idea.

She paced back to the table and sat down. "I assumed someone drove by, and that's what scared this person off. Then my neighbor called the police. Thankfully, there was a cop car close. First responders probably got here in less than five minutes."

She held her breath, waiting to see if Rafferty would fall for her excuse.

"I'd say you're very lucky then," he finally said.

Heidi released her breath. It appeared he'd

bought her story. "I wish I could say the same for Beau."

"We all do. I'll keep you updated. I'm sending some work over soon. One more thing: If the police start asking questions, whatever you do, don't share too much information. I don't need them poking around in my business. You've already created quite the headache for me. You know I like to stay off the radar, yet you gave them my name and number last night."

Indignation rose in her. "I didn't know what to say when they questioned me. But I tried to handle it the best way I could."

"Try harder."

The line went dead.

She pressed her eyes closed as she mentally replayed the conversation.

Thinking of what Rafferty had said and what he hadn't said.

She had so many mounting questions.

Suddenly, she felt restless.

Maybe it was partially due to the fact she was trapped in this house. Maybe the whole idea that she wasn't allowed to leave made her want to leave.

Wasn't there some kind of psychology behind that? She wasn't sure.

But all she wanted to do right now was to take a walk. Get some fresh air. Clear her head.

Instead, she glanced at her computer and remembered she had work to do.

She opened her laptop and skimmed her emails.

Her gaze stopped at one from Howard Monarch. What could Mr. Monarch want?

Something about the man had always given her bad vibes. He owned a tech firm, and he'd hired Rafferty's men on many occasions to act as personal security.

He must have lots of threats to his life if he needed bodyguards. But it seemed strange because she'd talked to him on occasion and the man came across as so low-key, like the type who didn't like attention and who liked to keep mostly to himself.

Heidi clicked on the email, curious as to what he had to say to her now.

———

Stephen sat in the driver's seat of a white van with *Ronnie's Drywall and Plaster* written on the sides. It was parked on the side of the neighborhood street—but only as a cover.

Gage Pearson, one of his new colleagues, was

with him. They both wore coveralls over their tactical pants and black T-shirts.

They were here to keep an eye on Heidi's house.

More than anything, he wanted to go inside and see for himself that she was okay. But he couldn't. Not only was it too risky, but Rafferty already had another one of his men stationed outside.

If worse came to worst, he and Gage could go to the door and pretend to be there to fix up her place after last night's fire.

But there was always the chance he'd be recognized.

From where he sat in the van, Stephen saw the new bodyguard sitting in an SUV in front of Heidi's place. It was Donald Jackson, another former colleague.

One he didn't hold in high esteem. The man was too much of a hothead.

All muscle, little substance. The guy often didn't use words. He used brute strength instead.

Stephen blew out a long breath.

His mind had been racing ever since everything happened yesterday. Instead of finding answers, he'd found more questions. Who had left those bugs and the camera in Heidi's house? Rafferty? If so, why? So he could keep an eye on her and make sure she was loyal to him?

His stomach roiled at the thought.

"Who do you think killed Beau?" Gage asked. "You've had some time to think about it now. Any theories?"

"I can't honestly say who it was." He needed more information first on Beau's latest assignments. On his enemies.

He needed information on Rafferty.

There were too many holes that had to be filled before anything would make sense.

"Just so you know, it wasn't one of our guys from the Shadow Agency. That's not how we operate."

The Shadow Agency was the company Gage worked for—and now Stephen also. It operated similar to Blackstone, only they took assignments that didn't require setting their morals aside.

"I never thought it was one of us. I also don't think it was one of my former colleagues at Blackstone."

Gage's gaze remained on Heidi's townhouse. "So then, who was it?"

"I wish I knew. Maybe we all have enemies we didn't even know about coming out of the woodwork."

Stephen shifted in his seat, tired of sitting here doing nothing. Yet he wouldn't leave—he had to know Heidi was safe.

The minutes ticked by.

"Any updates on Larchmont?" Stephen asked.

Alan Larchmont headed up the Shadow Agency. He was the one in ICU after a device implanted near his own heart had caused damage.

"Last I heard, he's still in a coma," Gage said. "I'm not sure if he'll come out of it or not."

"Any updates on Cynthia?" Cynthia was Larchmont's wife—only none of Larchmont's guys had known she existed until she arrived at the hospital and began calling the shots.

Even though Stephen didn't have a history with the team, he could see where her showing up would be unsettling.

"We have a couple of guys looking into her background," Gage said. "It turns out she was a lobbyist for military reform. Before that, she had a multimillion-dollar hair care company she sold for a huge payout."

"So she's been the one financing the Shadow Agency?"

"Seems like a good guess. She's also Larchmont's top advisor."

"But he kept her a secret, you said?"

Gage shrugged. "My guess is so he could protect her."

"I suppose that makes sense."

"She's a force to be reckoned with in her own right."

Too many secrets made everything feel uncertain. Now the whole agency was in peril.

Two hours into their surveillance, Donald opened the door to his SUV.

Stephen sat up straighter.

The man stretched before starting toward Heidi's house.

"What is he doing?" Stephen muttered.

At once, images of the man doing something horrible to Heidi filled his mind. What if Donald was heading inside to finish off Heidi? What if Rafferty decided to get rid of anyone he considered disposable?

Stephen reached for the door handle when Gage's hand came down on his shoulder. "Not yet."

His heart pounded in his ears. "What do you mean? We don't know what he's planning to do."

Stephen continued to watch as Donald walked toward the front door. He saw the gun at the man's side. He knew what that man was capable of.

"Let's just wait a minute," Gage said. "We don't want to show our hand yet."

"But if we wait too long, Heidi could die."

Stephen's words hung in the air as time seemed to stand still.

CHAPTER
NINE

HEIDI HEARD the brisk knock at her door and slammed her laptop closed.

Her heart raced, almost as if she'd been caught doing something wrong.

But she hadn't been. She'd simply been reading a message from Monarch.

Her head still spun from what he'd said.

He was trying to get in touch with Rafferty, but the man wasn't answering his phone. He wanted Heidi's help to contact him. He'd written: Tell him it's about the commander.

The commander? Who was the commander?

She didn't respond. Not yet.

She'd contact Rafferty first and see what he wanted her to say.

The knock sounded again.

Her attention shifted to the door.

Who was there? Was it Stephen? Hope filled her for a moment.

Then she heard, "Heidi. It's me, Donald. Open up."

A lump formed in her throat.

Donald? The man had always given her the creeps. There was something about the way he looked at her that left her uneasy.

And now he was here.

Should she open the door for him? Was it even safe for her to do so?

He rammed his fist into the wood again, and Heidi hated the fact he was making a scene. The last thing she wanted was any more attention to be drawn to her.

She quickly rose from her seat and rushed to the door. As she grasped the handle, she hesitated another moment. Then she drew in a deep breath to pull herself together and opened it.

Donald's lips quirked in annoyance as he stared at her with his bloodshot eyes.

He clearly hadn't gotten much sleep last night.

Or maybe he had a hangover. Rafferty had reprimanded him several times about drinking too much. Maybe that explained why his skin looked so fleshy and pale and why, despite the fact he was fit, he still had a pudge at his midsection.

"Is everything okay?" She was sure to keep her cool.

Without invitation, he stepped inside and closed the door behind him. "We gotta get out of here."

Her hands went to her hips. "What do you mean, we have to get out of here?"

"Rafferty said it's not safe for you to stay here anymore."

Panic raced through her. "Why? What's happening?"

"We don't know if the person who killed Beau is going to come back here and try to finish what he started. We need to get you somewhere safe."

"Where would we go?" Her heart thumped harder in her chest. She couldn't stand the thought of going anywhere with Donald. She didn't trust the man.

"I don't know. Rafferty is going to send me the address. I'm just doing what he said."

"Why didn't he tell me himself?" She was stalling for time, wasn't she?

She hadn't even realized what she was doing, but it made sense. Though . . . she wasn't sure how stalling would help. Was she hoping Stephen would magically show up and step in?

She only had herself to depend on right now. She needed to get any other ideas out of her head.

Donald snorted. "Who do I look like? A mind reader? You know Rafferty. He says to do something, and he expects you to do it. No questions asked. That's why I'm here right now."

Heidi couldn't deny his words. That was the way that Rafferty worked.

But she couldn't bring herself to move. Maybe her home wasn't safe, but it was her home. Besides, if things went south, how would Stephen find her? She'd be on her own.

She liked having options.

Donald let out a long sigh. "I don't know why you're standing there. Go get an overnight bag together. We need to get out of here."

What should she do? Comply?

Heidi didn't have much choice. If she refused to go, then Rafferty would know something was up. Though he'd never made her feel threatened, she knew what the man was capable of.

If she went with Donald, maybe it would buy her some time.

She swallowed the lump in her throat and nodded. "Give me a minute to grab a few things."

As she hurried toward her room, she prayed she didn't regret this.

———

Stephen's hand remained on the van door.

More than anything, he wanted to rush outside and check on Heidi.

Not because he really knew the woman. Sure, they'd had some fun chatting in the past. Maybe they'd even teased each other on occasion. But that was as far as it had gone.

However, she was clearly the victim here. She'd been looking for a job, and she'd accepted the wrong one. There was no way she could have known what she was getting herself into.

Rafferty had taken advantage of an innocent woman.

Stephen saw the door open.

Donald and Heidi stepped out. Heidi had a small backpack over her shoulder as Donald gripped her arm.

He glanced around as if looking for trouble before escorting her to the Suv parked out front.

As he did, Heidi looked over at the van. Though the windows of the van were tinted, Stephen somehow felt as if she could see him. As if she knew he was there.

Maybe it was foolish. But maybe it wasn't.

"What do you think?" Stephen didn't pull his

gaze off Heidi.

"I think we need to follow them," Gage muttered.

"You sure we shouldn't just go stop them before they leave? What if he tries to—"

"If he tries to do anything, we'll be right behind them," Gage said. "We'll stop it before it happens."

Stephen nodded, knowing his colleague's words were true.

He waited until the car pulled away before cranking the van's engine.

He'd been well trained in tailing people, so he should be able to do this without drawing any attention.

Problem was, so had Donald.

Stephen couldn't let Donald know he was being followed. That would only cause his former colleague to react. Maybe even do something desperate.

Stephen needed to play this carefully—more carefully than he'd ever played anything before.

Lord, please protect Heidi. Don't let anything happen to her. And give me the wisdom to do what I need to do to help.

CHAPTER
TEN

HEIDI COULDN'T IGNORE the tremble raking through her as she sat beside Donald in the front seat of the black SUV.

Where was he taking her?

She'd glanced down the street before they left and had spotted a white work van a few houses down. She didn't know why, but she wondered if Stephen was inside.

Maybe it was wishful thinking, but she hoped that was the case. Otherwise, she was in this all alone.

"Where are we going?" Her tight chest rendered her voice breathless.

Donald gripped the steering wheel and didn't even bother to look at her.

He had AirPods in his ears, and she was nearly

certain someone was feeding him directions on the phone. Every once in a while, he muttered something indiscernible.

He drove entirely too fast for the neighborhood. Zipping around corners. Not stopping at stop signs. It wasn't safe.

However, nothing felt safe right now. Heidi didn't foresee that changing anytime soon either.

"Where are we going?" she repeated.

"You'll see when we get there."

She hated feeling helpless. Feeling like this was out of her control.

But now that she was in the car with Donald, she didn't know how to change course.

She pressed her eyes shut. *Dear Lord, please help me. Protect me.*

Praying was the best thing she could do right now. She'd learned to rely on God after her mom's accident. Before that, she'd felt lost at times, even empty and unsure what she believed.

She'd turned to academics. Had gotten a full-ride scholarship to UGA to study business. She'd been on the right track to success.

But seeing her mom suffer had brought Heidi to her knees. She'd cried out to God, begging Him to help her.

And He had. He hadn't healed her mom, but

He'd helped bring Heidi peace. She'd begun to read her Bible and pray. She'd found a nearby church and had joined a Bible study.

She'd even had what she called her "guardian angel" watching out for her. On more than one occasion, she'd felt danger around her. Once a man had followed her from the grocery store only to disappear after she rounded the corner.

Another time a man had pounded on the door outside her house, acting as if he might break the structure down. But he'd eventually left.

Still another time the pipes had broken at her house, and she wasn't sure how she would pay for the repairs. The next morning, an envelope with five hundred dollars cash had been left outside.

Every time something like that happened, she thought she heard someone humming in the distance.

Her guardian angel.

She wasn't sure she would have gotten through her mother's accident and death without God.

She wouldn't get through this without Him either.

Trying not to be too obvious, she glanced behind her.

At first, she didn't see the white van. She thought

maybe she'd misinterpreted the entire situation when she left her house.

Then the vehicle appeared several cars back. Far enough away that no one else should notice.

"What are you looking at?" Donald barked, glancing behind him. "You see something?"

Heidi scolded herself. What was she thinking? She should be a better actress than this.

She might just sabotage her one chance of being helped.

"I'm just nervous," she told him. "You made it sound as if someone could be coming after us right now."

"You see something I don't?"

Heidi shook her head. "No. Like I said, I'm just nervous."

"You don't be nervous. Let me handle this."

Yet she had no confidence Donald could handle this situation.

She hoped her gut instinct was correct and that was Stephen in the white van back there. But she had no way to tell for certain.

As they continued down the road farther from her house, Heidi realized she could be headed away from the only life she'd ever known.

———

"Where is he taking her?" Stephen muttered as he stared at the interstate in front of him. It was busy with cars weaving in and out.

"I have no idea," Gage said. "But Heidi is okay for now. Let's just keep following them."

Stephen intended on doing just that. But that didn't mean he liked this situation. Not at all.

He should have tried to contact her this morning. Should have reached out some way to let her know she wasn't alone in this.

But he'd never expected Rafferty to make this move. He should have known better.

Heidi had to be frantic.

Stephen's gaze shifted to a gray Camry three vehicles in front of them. "Is it just me or is that guy sticking with Donald also?"

"You mean the gray sedan? I noticed too. Let's keep an eye on it."

Had Rafferty sent another of his men to make sure that Heidi made it safely to wherever he wanted her to go?

Stephen wouldn't put it past the man.

Unless . . . it was someone with other intentions.

He kept an eye on both vehicles as they headed away from the metropolitan area and toward a rural area. Where in the world was Donald taking Heidi?

The farther away from the city they got, the

harder it would be to remain concealed, especially since there was less traffic.

Twenty minutes later, Donald turned off the main road onto a two-lane road leading past several old farms to the northwest of the city.

The gray car turned also.

Stephen gripped the wheel tightly as he waited to see what would happen next.

As if to answer that question, the gray sedan suddenly accelerated.

The driver charged toward Donald's vehicle.

"What the . . ." Gage muttered.

The next instant, the gray car pulled into the other lane . . . and rammed into the side of Donald's SUV, sending it barreling off the road.

CHAPTER
ELEVEN

"DONALD!" Heidi yelled as the SUV veered to the side.

Then the vehicle bumped, bumped, bumped.

The tires had hit the shoulder.

She screamed and glanced at the gray car beside them. With its tinted windows she couldn't see inside.

Donald muttered something beneath his breath as he fought to keep control of his vehicle.

It was no use. The impact was too jarring.

The SUV tilted. Careened forward. Slammed into the oversized ditch running parallel to the road.

Heidi jerked forward, gasping as her seatbelt caught her. The airbag deployed, filling the space with white powder and making her lose her sense of place.

She coughed, sediment from the airbag filling her lungs.

Donald . . .

She glanced in his direction. But it was impossible to see him past the airbag.

Smoke filled the air, and Heidi coughed again before calling, "Donald?"

There was no answer. Had he passed out? Or was he . . . dead?

The scent of smoke grew stronger.

She swallowed back a cry.

Heidi had to get out of this car. Now.

———

Stephen watched as the Camry sped away. He immediately turned his gaze back to the SUV Heidi was in.

It had veered into a ditch and hit the edge hard.

Smoke poured from beneath the hood.

It was only a matter of time before the whole thing went up in flames.

He squealed to a stop behind the SUV. Throwing his vehicle into Park, he and Gage wasted no time climbing out.

They ran to Heidi's door, jerked it open, and

heard her raspy cough. The airbag jostled as she frantically clawed at it.

She was alive! Praise the Lord. The air left his lungs as relief filled him. But the feeling only lasted a minute.

He had to get her out.

"It's me. Stephen. Let's get you out of here." He grabbed the utility knife from his pocket and cut her seatbelt off.

She coughed again as she said his name. When he tugged her from the seat, she practically collapsed into his arms.

He gathered her to his chest and carried her away from the SUV.

As he did that, Gage ran to the other side and tried to open the door.

"It's stuck," he muttered.

Stephen laid Heidi behind the van, where she'd be safe. Then he raced back to the SUV to help Gage.

A new smell filled the air. Not just smoke. This time it was also . . . gas.

"We don't have much time," he yelled to Gage.

Gage tugged at the door again. "Let's go to the other side and see if we can pull him out."

Stephen sprinted to the passenger side. As soon as he opened the door, the scent of gasoline grew even stronger.

He took a step back. "I don't know about this, Gage."

Gage ran around to meet him and paused. "There's a gas leak. Stephen, we've got to get away."

He stared inside the SUV. Donald still wasn't moving, yelling, or trying to help himself. He must be passed out. Unless he hadn't made it.

"Stephen . . ." Gage grabbed his arm and tugged him back.

Reluctantly, Stephen and Gage hurried back toward the van.

Just as they ducked behind the vehicle, the SUV exploded, sending waves of heat and debris crashing through the air.

CHAPTER
TWELVE

HEART POUNDING OUT OF CONTROL, Heidi crawled on her hands and knees. She peered around the van and watched as Stephen and his friend tried to rescue Donald.

Then they paused. Took a step back.

And started to run.

The next instant, an explosion ripped through the air.

She muffled a scream as she covered her head.

What about Stephen? And the man who'd been with him? Were they okay?

As the flames died down, she lifted her head.

Stephen and his friend crouched in front of her . . . unharmed.

Thank God!

She offered him a nod to let him know she was fine.

"I need to see if Donald is still alive!" he yelled.

A moment later, Stephen and his friend darted toward the burning SUV.

In her gut, Heidi knew it was too late. There was no way the man had survived that explosion. Still, they needed to know for sure.

Stephen and the other man returned a moment later. They both had grim looks in their eyes. Donald was dead.

Her heart panged with grief.

"We've got to get out of here." Stephen took Heidi's arm and helped her to her feet. "Are you okay?"

"All things considered, yes."

"Then we need to go." He nodded toward the van. "Now."

Sirens sounded in the distance. Someone must have either seen the fire or heard the explosion and called it in. Or maybe Donald's vehicle had an alert system that let people know when an accident occurred. She couldn't be sure.

Either way, Heidi knew she didn't want to stay here. What if the gray sedan came back? She couldn't risk that.

Stephen helped her into the van. Then he and his

colleague climbed inside also, and they took off down the road, in the opposite direction of the sirens.

She looked at the remains of the SUV as they drove past. Flames still flared from the hood. The airbags were charred but blocked the sight of anything inside—including the backpack she'd grabbed before leaving her home. Smoke rose from the open door.

Someone had tried to kill both her and Donald. She couldn't stop thinking about that fact.

They'd succeeded in taking Donald out—permanently. Heidi may not have liked the man, but she hadn't wanted this either.

The whole situation could have turned out so much differently. Stephen had come for her. Saved her life.

Maybe she could trust him after all.

But she still had a lot of questions he had yet to answer.

Stephen stared at the road, double checking to make sure the gray sedan didn't return. That the driver didn't come back to inspect his work.

So far, the coast was clear.

The wailing sirens remained behind them, so they shouldn't cross paths with any emergency vehicles.

"I'm so glad you guys showed up when you did." Heidi leaned forward from the back seat to speak with them.

"Me too." Stephen's jaw hardened as he said the words.

That had been too close for comfort. If only one or two things were different, Heidi would be dead right now.

"This is Gage, by the way," Stephen said. "He's my new colleague."

"Thank you for being here." Heidi rubbed her arms as she drew in a shaky breath. "Where are we going?"

"We need to figure that out." Stephen gripped the wheel as he stared at the road ahead.

Gage was working on those details now. They needed to go somewhere they wouldn't be traced.

"If it wasn't Rafferty who tried to kill me, then who hired the person in the sedan? Who killed Beau? And threw the Molotov cocktail into my house?" Heidi's questions hung in the air.

"To be honest, I'm not really sure," Stephen told her.

"Won't Rafferty know you're helping me?" Alarm

filled Heidi's voice. "He's going to realize Donald is dead and that I'm not with him."

Stephen had already thought that one through. "He'll know *someone* grabbed you. Most likely, he'll think it was the person driving the sedan. He shouldn't know it was us."

"Good point." She blew out a breath. "That will buy us a little time."

Her words were spoken like a true operative. She'd obviously been working in this business for a while—for too long maybe.

Despite that, he was impressed by her level-headedness in the situation.

But her question was excellent.

Who was behind this? And why did they want Heidi dead?

CHAPTER
THIRTEEN

AN HOUR AND A HALF LATER, Heidi watched as they pulled up to an ordinary-looking ranch-style house at the end of a long lane in the middle of the woods.

She wasn't sure what she'd been expecting, but it wasn't this.

Stephen stopped in front of the attached garage and put the van in Park. "Trevor, another colleague, secured this place for us. We should be safe here for a while."

For a while? That indicated there might be an end in sight. But Heidi doubted that.

It seemed this would only end in one way: death.

Maybe hers. Maybe Stephen's. She wasn't sure.

Either way, she shivered at the thought.

"Let's get inside," Stephen said. "We can talk more there."

Heidi was grateful when he waited for her outside the van. That he took her arm.

She wasn't sure she could stand on her own right now. All her muscles felt wobbly, and her head was spinning. That wasn't to mention the fact she smelled like smoke. White dust was sprinkled across her nose —and probably other places. She'd discovered a small scratch on her arm.

All those things made her realize just how close she'd come to losing her life.

As everything sank in, Stephen escorted her inside.

The house was plain with the bare minimum of furniture and no notable decorations.

That was fine. It didn't matter.

They just needed somewhere to regroup.

As soon as they were inside, Stephen led her to a small kitchen table. He didn't let go of her arm until she was seated.

Stephen and Gage sat across from her. She observed Gage a moment. He was probably Stephen's age, with dark hair and grayish eyes.

He'd been in the military also, hadn't he? Except he hadn't left with Rafferty. That was her best guess.

Stephen wasted no time getting down to business. "We need to figure out what's going on."

"I'd love nothing more than to do that also. I don't even know where to start from here." Just as she said the words, her phone rang.

She grabbed it from her pocket and glanced at the screen. Her pulse kicked up a beat.

"It's Rafferty," she muttered. "What should I do?"

———

Stephen's gut clenched. "I didn't realize you had your phone. You need to turn it off. Now."

Heidi's eyes widened. "I . . . I would have earlier. But it's untraceable. And—"

"Who told you it was untraceable?" Stephen took it from her hand and slid the battery out.

"Rafferty . . ." As the word left her lips, the conviction in her voice faltered.

They all knew Rafferty couldn't be trusted. Just because he said something was untraceable didn't mean it actually was.

"Even if it is untraceable, we need to buy some time." Stephen set the lifeless phone back on the table, praying Rafferty hadn't already tracked them. "Let Rafferty think someone grabbed you."

"You don't think he'll suspect it's you?"

Stephen exchanged a look with Gage before they both shook their heads.

"He shouldn't." Gage ran a hand through his hair, tension in his gaze. "We've been careful to cover our tracks. There's no way he should know we're with you."

"Especially now that the tracking devices have been removed from our shoulders," Stephen added.

Her eyes widened at his words. "What?"

Stephen nodded grimly. "We were subject to different kinds of experiments. One of them was having GPS trackers planted inside us so our every move could be monitored. As I mentioned earlier, we also had devices implanted near our hearts. We were supposedly living free, but we weren't actually free at all."

"I can't imagine," she muttered. "It's horrifying to think these people did those things without your permission."

"We're still uncovering everything that was done to us while we were in 'training' for Project Elevate," Stephen said.

Heidi tilted her head in confusion. "What's Project Elevate?"

Stephen and Gage exchanged another look.

"We were handpicked for certain experiments the military wanted to do on an elite group of soldiers,"

Stephen explained. "They purposefully chose people who didn't have any strong community connections."

"Why would that be important?" she asked.

"Because without any connections, if something went wrong, there would be fewer people to notice and to keep them accountable for it," Stephen said.

"That explains it . . ." Heidi slowly shook her head.

"They were trying to develop a super soldier, of sorts," Gage continued.

"I've heard about stuff like that, but I thought it was only fiction." She paused. "I figured you guys were Special Ops or maybe even Black Ops."

"We were . . . kind of." Stephen frowned. "Only Rafferty took it to the next level."

Heidi sighed and leaned back. "How many of you are there?"

"We're not sure about that either," Stephen said. "We're still trying to uncover everything. Rafferty was initially the scientist in charge of the program, but he was fired. When that happened, he took some of his guys with him and started his own security firm."

"Blackstone." Heidi slowly nodded as she took in each detail.

"There could have been other groups of soldiers

who came through before my group," Stephen said. "We're not sure. Gage and his crew came later."

She glanced at Gage. "What happened to the rest of you?"

"We were recruited into the program under a different leader," Gage said. "Most of us stuck with the program and did covert missions. Missions where, if we were caught, the government would claim no connection with us."

"They can do that?"

Gage nodded. "They can, and they did."

"That's awful." She shook her head. "Who even approved this program?"

"We never questioned it," Stephen said. "We knew it was all top-secret and were taught not to ask questions. We were almost brainwashed into thinking that way."

"Eventually, the program was shut down," Gage continued. "The guys who trained with me went to work for a man named Alan Larchmont."

"Does this Larchmont guy have answers?" Heidi asked. "Someone needs accountability for all this."

The events of the past few weeks replayed in Stephen's mind. "Maybe he does have answers, but apparently he also had a device implanted near his heart. He's still in ICU in a coma, so we can't ask him any questions right now."

Silence stretched a moment, and Heidi shook her head. "None of this seems real, yet I know it is. I learned early on that it was better not to ask too many questions. So that's what I tried to do. Now I can see that was a mistake."

"You couldn't have known," Stephen murmured. "None of us did. None of us knew the extent of what was going on."

Heidi let out another sigh before sitting up straight again. "So what do we do now?"

"That's an excellent question," Stephen said.

Heidi's eyes lit. "I forgot. I have an update for you. With everything else that's happened, it slipped my mind."

"An update?" Maybe this would be something useful.

Even more than that fact, Stephen felt satisfaction stretch through him.

Heidi was beginning to trust him even more.

That was exactly what they needed right now—to trust each other if they were going to get through this.

CHAPTER
FOURTEEN

HEIDI DREW in a deep breath as she wrestled with her thoughts. As she wrestled with each new bit of information. As she wrestled with comprehending the scope of what was going on.

"I wish I had my computer with me, and I could be a little more precise. I had it with me in the car with Donald when—" Her voice cracked, and she couldn't finish the statement.

She didn't want to think about Donald. The only thing that brought her comfort was in knowing he'd been unconscious after the accident. That meant he hadn't known the explosion was coming. Maybe he hadn't suffered.

"What about this update?" Stephen narrowed his eyes as he studied her.

"I got an email from Monarch."

Stephen and Gage exchanged another glance.

"He's desperate to get in touch with Rafferty, but it sounds like Rafferty is ghosting him. I know the two are as thick as thieves. They talk all the time. I can't help but feel like something is wrong."

Stephen frowned, his gaze hardening. "I worked Monarch's protective detail more than once. The man is either powerful, doing something illegal and damaging, or both."

"From what I remember, he faced numerous threats from people who weren't happy with him and his business," Heidi told them.

"That is interesting, but I'm not sure how his email will help us," Stephen said.

"There's more." Heidi squirmed in the uncomfortable wooden chair. "He mentioned that he needed to talk to Rafferty about the commander."

"Who is the commander?" Gage asked. "Commander Davis?"

"That's the thing. I have no idea." She raised her palms up, showing they were empty, that she had no answers.

Stephen's eyes narrowed. "It seems weird that he would mention that to you, almost like he wanted to say just enough to scare Rafferty into action."

"You're probably right. I thought the whole thing was strange." She withdrew her arms and crossed

them over her chest as she leaned back in the uncomfortable wooden chair.

"We need to figure out who this commander is."
Stephen tapped his finger on the table. "He could
have the answers we need."

"It's going to be hard to track him down if we
don't know any more information," Gage said.

Stephen glanced at Heidi again. "That's where
you can come in."

She slowly nodded. "Maybe. But I'm not sure
exactly what I can do."

"I've got a few ideas." Stephen's gaze locked onto
hers. "If you're willing."

"Let's hear them." At this point, Heidi had no
other choice.

If they didn't find out answers, they all could lose
their lives.

———

Stephen and Gage spent the next two hours
questioning Heidi. They tried to find out anything
she might know, even things she might not realize
she knew.

She knew the schedules of all the operatives.
Knew what kind of jobs they'd done. Knew where
several of them were now.

But unfortunately, she didn't share anything that helped them find Rafferty or figure out who the commander might be.

Finally, they took a break for lunch. Gage had brought a few groceries with him in the van. He carried them inside, and they made peanut butter sandwiches to eat with chips.

It was better than nothing.

Stephen knew they couldn't stay at this house long. Staying here wouldn't help them find the answers they so desperately needed.

What they needed was a game plan on how to find out more information. He'd hoped Heidi might be able to help with that—and she *had* been helpful.

Either way, bringing Rafferty down was one of their first priorities. Until he was taken care of, he would remain a threat to all the men who'd been through Project Elevate. Plus, there was the fact other men were out there, men who had flunked out of the program because of compromised moral compasses.

Those were the men who'd do anything Rafferty asked. That made them dangerous, especially considering their skillsets.

"You guys, we've got a problem," Gage muttered as he stood near the window.

Stephen rose from his seat. "What's going on?"

"There's movement outside."

Heidi sucked in a breath. "Did those men find us here?"

"Someone did."

"How is that even possible?" Stephen muttered.

"We'll figure that out later." Gage dropped the curtain and hurried back toward them. "Right now, we need to get out of here."

"Should we head to the van?" Heidi asked.

"No, we're going to have to escape on foot," Gage said. "And we need to leave now."

FIFTEEN

PANIC RACED THROUGH HEIDI.

How would they have been found? Had the fact she had her phone on her led these guys straight to their location?

She prayed that wasn't the case. That one decision wouldn't be a death sentence for them all. She should have been thinking things through more, but it hadn't occurred to her at the time.

Stephen grabbed her arm and pulled her toward the back of the house. He'd paused only long enough to scoop up his backpack and shove his laptop in it.

Gage waited for them at the back of the house, peering out the window.

"Do you see anyone?" Stephen asked as they reached the back door.

"They're not back here yet, but they will be.

We've got to go. Lie low so they don't know we're onto them."

Stephen turned toward Heidi. "I need you to do everything I say. Your life depends on it. Understand?"

Fear pulsed through her, but she nodded. "I understand."

"Let's go." Gage opened the door and stepped out first.

He held his gun as he scanned everything around them. Then he gave them a nod.

Stephen followed Gage across the yard, gripping Heidi's arm.

They darted toward the woods. The mid-October trees filling the space appeared surprisingly threadbare. Leaves had only started falling a few days ago. She prayed the remaining foliage would conceal their presence.

Stephen moved fast, pulling her into the woods. Dodging trees. Motioning for her to watch her steps.

More than anything, she wanted to glance back. To see if those men noticed them yet.

But she didn't dare.

They ran at full speed for what felt like hours. In truth, it was probably ten or fifteen minutes.

She'd lost her breath about five minutes into their

escape. Yet it seemed as if Gage and Stephen still weren't even winded.

Were they safe yet?

Heidi needed a breather. But before she could ask Stephen to slow down, a yell sounded in the distance.

She sucked in a breath.

She knew this was far from being over, especially when Stephen tightened his grip on her and picked up speed.

————

Stephen was grateful they'd gotten as far as they had. He'd known it was iffy they'd even be able to get this far away.

After another few minutes, they paused.

"Let's split up," Gage said. "I'll go to the left and try to distract them. Meanwhile, you get her somewhere safe."

"Split up?" The question sounded breathless as Heidi gulped in air. "Are you sure that's a good idea?"

Stephen didn't have time to comfort her or reassure her now. "That will work. I have a satellite phone on me. We should be able to stay in contact. We'll meet up again once we know it's safe."

"Copy that." Gage nodded to his right. "Go."

Stephen released her arm then grasped her hand. Then he pulled her through the rocky wilderness while Gage took off in the opposite direction.

This time, they moved even faster—as fast as possible given the uneven terrain.

They dodged trees and branches and rocks. Crossed a small stream. Scaled a small rock wall.

He kept his ears attuned to everything happening around him.

Stephen thought their plan had worked. Thought the guys had followed Gage instead of them.

He prayed Gage wouldn't be caught, wouldn't be hurt. Gage was an excellent operative. If anyone could do this, he could.

Stephen glanced beside him at Heidi as they ran. Saw how her cheeks were flushed. How her breathing came shallow and fast.

This was all a lot, and he wasn't sure how much farther Heidi would be able to run.

Maybe they could pause a moment.

Just as the thought crossed his mind, a stick cracked in the distance.

His muscles tensed.

Had one of the operatives come this way after all?

He couldn't take that chance.

"We need to take cover," he whispered to Heidi. He spotted a rocky overhang. "Over here."

Running was too risky right now. The guy was too close. He'd see them, hear them. Hiding was the only choice.

Stephen stashed Heidi in the small space, climbed beneath the rock, and squeezed in beside her.

Then he gripped his gun and waited.

CHAPTER
SIXTEEN

HEIDI'S HEART pounded with such force her pulse was all she could hear.

Someone still followed them, didn't they? What would this person do if he discovered her and Stephen hiding here?

Part of her didn't want to think about it. But how could she not?

The only comfort she found was in knowing Stephen was beside her. He crouched, fully alert, with his gun drawn.

She thought they were out of sight. The rocky overhang was large enough that they remained in the shadows. But if this guy looked hard enough, he would see them.

Then all she could do was pray for the best.

As another stick snapped, she pressed her eyes closed. *Please, Lord . . . watch over us. Protect us.*

The steps came closer. Closer.

She tried to push herself as far into the crevice as she could.

Because there was one thing she knew for sure.

These men were trained and dangerous.

These were the same guys who'd killed Beau. Who'd run her and Donald off the road, ultimately killing him. They'd probably wanted to kill her too. In fact, she would probably be dead right now if it wasn't for Stephen and Gage.

They'd protected her once. Now she needed to believe they could protect her again.

The footsteps came to a stop. A shadow stretched across the ground.

This guy had paused directly in front of the rocky overhang.

All he needed to do was bend down and he'd see them.

Then it would depend on who had the fastest trigger finger—Stephen or the man pursuing them.

Nausea swirled inside Heidi at the thought.

————

Stephen watched the man. He could only see the guy's black cargo pants and boots.

Not his face.

Was this man a former colleague? He had no idea if this was someone he'd recognize or not.

Stephen still wasn't sure who these guys worked for. Though Rafferty seemed to be the most obvious choice, there were no certainties.

Besides, why would Rafferty send two of his own guys to protect Heidi, and then send more guys to kill them?

It didn't make sense.

Unless Rafferty's goal was to silence them all.

There were still other things that didn't make sense.

How had they been found? He'd taken the battery from her phone.

But what if Rafferty had other ways of tracking her, just like he'd had other ways of tracking Stephen and his colleagues?

The thought made his blood go ice cold.

Stephen tried to recall any jewelry she might be wearing, but he didn't remember any. Rafferty wouldn't put it in her clothing since that was changed too often to be effective.

Then what?

His thoughts continued to race.

Would Rafferty have gone so far as to put a tracking device in Heidi's body like he'd done to them?

His gut lurched. He hated the thought of it. But right now, it was the only thing that made sense.

He would need to check.

First, he needed to figure out what this guy in front of him would do.

The man was so close Stephen could hear him breathing.

Even though Stephen and Heidi were in the shadows, they could still be discovered.

What about Gage? Was he okay?

Stephen tried to think everything through and plan his next move to cover all the what-ifs.

His heart pounded in his ears as he waited, his finger poised on the trigger of his gun.

A moment later, the guy took another step. And another.

Away from where they were hiding.

Just far enough for Stephen to get a look at his face. The man had dark hair that was curly, a lean frame, and sharp eyes.

Stephen had never seen the guy before.

However, the man was looking at his phone.

Almost as if following a tracker.

CHAPTER
SEVENTEEN

WHAT WAS THAT GUY DOING? Heidi mused.

She'd caught a glimpse of his face. He didn't look familiar. Not like one of Rafferty's guys. However, he had hired a few new ones she hadn't met yet.

Why was he looking at his phone right now? Did he even have any service out here?

Stephen tensed beside her. He was clearly on edge —as he should be.

Her heart still pounded in her ears as she tried to anticipate what would happen.

The next instant, the man raised his phone higher as if searching for a signal.

Then he began to pace away.

It was too early to relax. However, she *did* blow out the breath she'd been holding.

This seemed like a good sign at least.

As the man kept pacing away, she and Stephen remained where they were.

Even after the man disappeared from sight, they stayed there. Unmoving. Silent. Nearly frozen.

"Shouldn't we run?" she whispered.

He moved away from her slightly and shook his head.

Then his gaze met hers. "I'm going to tell you something, and it's going to sound crazy."

"I don't know if things can sound any crazier than they already have been."

His gaze still remained tense. "Did you ever have to make any doctor's visits or medical appointments as a part of your job? Appointments for yourself?"

"I had a physical when I first got the job." She narrowed her eyes. "How is that important though?"

"They didn't have to put you to sleep or anything?"

"No, it was just a basic appointment. I don't understand why you're asking."

"Since you started working for Rafferty, have you had to have any type of procedures where you had to be put under?"

Her confusion only grew as she tried to think it through. "I haven't had any surgeries or anything." Then a memory hit her. "Except . . ."

"Except what?"

"I was sedated once for a root canal. A couple of years ago. But what does that have to do with any of this?"

"I'm afraid that one of the same trackers like Rafferty put in us might have been put in you also."

Her gut instantly tightened. "What?"

"I know it sounds unnerving."

"It doesn't just sound unnerving. It *is* unnerving."

"Do you remember being sore after the procedure? Or any unusual bruising?"

"They did tell me I started to flail. One of the hygienists had to press on my shoulders to hold me still so I didn't hurt myself or anyone else. You think it was something else, though, don't you?"

Stephen nodded grimly.

"Is that how those guys found us?" she asked as she absently rubbed her shoulders.

Was there something implanted beneath her skin?

"That's my best guess. I think the only reason that man didn't find us at our location is because this rock blocked any signal."

Her thoughts raced ahead. "But as soon as we leave this spot . . ."

He grimaced. "There's a good chance he'll find us."

Her gaze locked with his. "We can't let that happen."

"I know."

"So what are we going to do?" Her mind continued to race, to try to figure out a solution.

How else could they block this signal?

When she saw Stephen's gaze flicker to her shoulder, she realized exactly what he was thinking.

Nausea roiled inside her.

She turned as the contents of her stomach spewed from her mouth.

———

Stephen had sensed Heidi's stress even before she'd thrown up, and he wanted nothing more than to ease her mind. But that wasn't possible.

The situation was dire right now, especially if his suspicions were correct.

"I wouldn't ask you to do this unless I really felt our lives depended on it," he said.

"You want to cut this tracker out of me right here? Right now?" Heidi's voice pitched higher. "You don't even know for sure it's there."

"It's the only thing that makes sense. Can I see your right shoulder?"

She stared at him a moment before nodding. "Why not?"

She tugged the shoulder of her shirt down to allow Stephen to see her skin.

He pulled out his phone and used the flashlight so he could see better in the shadows.

He touched a small scar that almost looked like a freckle located in the same area where his tracker had been. Most people probably wouldn't notice it. They might think it looked like a small blemish or freckle even.

But Stephen knew exactly what it was.

"What do you see?" Her voice cracked.

"It looks like something was injected right here." He gently touched the spot on her shoulder.

"They can just inject these things?"

"The technology is amazing . . . and terrifying."

"I can't believe this." Her hand went to her stomach as if she might get sick again.

He squeezed her forearm, desperate to comfort her. "If we leave this inside you, then Rafferty—and whoever else has access to this tracker—will be able to follow you wherever you go."

"Why would he do this?"

"Because he thrives on control, and he doesn't care if he has anyone's permission."

She swallowed hard, looking unusually pale. "I'm not feeling so well."

Then she turned and threw up again.

He glanced away, giving her space.

He wished there was another solution. He really did. But there wasn't.

There was nothing he could do to make this better. Or less painful.

He feebly offered, "I'd give you a napkin, but I don't have one on me."

"It's okay." Heidi took a shaky breath, wiping her mouth with the sleeve of her sweatshirt.

"When I used to be a cage fighter, I always braced myself to get through each fight by controlling my breathing and picturing myself on a beach with no one else around."

"Wait—you were a cage fighter?" Surprise laced her voice.

"I turned to it to numb my pain. Anything seemed better than facing my future. I don't recommend it." He offered a feeble smile.

She smiled back before glancing at her shoulder again. "I need to get this thing out of me. How big is it?"

"Big enough to hurt coming out. It's not going to feel good," he warned her. "But I'll be as fast as I can."

She squeezed her eyes shut. "Don't tell me anything else. Just do it."

Stephen stared at her another moment, still hesitant to move forward.

Then he reached into his pocket. He pulled out a knife and a lighter to sterilize it with.

He wasn't looking forward to this.

But Rafferty had left them with no other choice.

CHAPTER
EIGHTEEN

HEIDI LIKED to think she was tough. But she knew she wasn't. Maybe she was mentally tough, and she could do challenging things within an office environment.

But having a tracker cut out of her without any anesthesia was *not* on her list of things she wanted to conquer.

Stephen had given her a stick to bite down on, and she was glad for that. Otherwise, she would have cried out.

Tears had streamed down her face as the blade cut into her skin.

Thankfully, Stephen was fast and efficient.

A few seconds later, he held out his knife. A small metal chip rested on the bloody blade.

She blinked as she stared at the small device.

She took the stick from her mouth and saw that she'd left teeth impressions on it. But it was better than crying out.

"It's so small," she muttered.

"That's all it takes." He looked back at her shoulder. "I don't have anything to bandage you up with right now. The cut is small, though—less than an inch."

"I'll be okay." Her skin felt tingly and sore, but the pain wasn't unbearable, especially now that it was over.

Later, she'd want to put some antiseptic on the wound. For now, she put pressure on it to stop the bleeding.

"What now?" Heidi stared up at Stephen.

Why did she think he had all the answers? She knew why. It was because he *did* seem to have all the answers. He knew what he was doing in this situation, and she found immense comfort in that fact.

"I'm going to make sure I leave this tracker somewhere far away from us. In fact, I need you to stay here a moment. I'm going to run up the hill and throw it in the opposite direction of where we're headed. That should buy us a little more time."

As worry surged through her, Heidi grabbed his arm. "Are you sure? What if they catch you?"

"I'm sure." His voice was unwavering. "I'll be careful."

She stared at him another moment before nodding.

Then Stephen handed her one of his guns. He'd brought two. "But hold onto this just in case."

She stared at the weapon, her hands suddenly trembling. Or maybe they'd been trembling all along, and she just hadn't noticed. She wasn't sure. Either way, this whole situation had her on edge.

In the blink of an eye, Stephen darted away, and she was left under the rock overhang alone.

The silence suddenly felt unsettling.

She grasped the gun, pleading with God she wouldn't have to use it.

The minutes ticked by. How far had Stephen gone? In her mind, he would be there and back in five minutes.

The farther away he was, the better, she supposed.

Then she heard a stick crack.

Had that come from Stephen?

Or had it come from one of the guys following them?

―――――

Stephen heard another stick crack.

He looked up. Saw the man who'd been following them earlier.

The guy had appeared on the crest of a hill.

Had he been lingering in the area, waiting for a signal?

Maybe.

The good news was that the man hadn't spotted Stephen yet.

Stephen ducked behind a tree, his heart thudding against his chest.

The man stood between him and Heidi.

If the guy picked up on a signal, it would lead him south to where Stephen had left the tracker. But it would still be nearly impossible for Stephen to get back to Heidi without being spotted.

He needed to carefully think this through.

Right now, he'd stay put. But if the man appeared close to discovering Heidi's location, Stephen would be forced into action.

He peered around the tree and watched.

The guy paused again and glanced at his phone.

Then he glanced to the left and right before finally starting north.

All Stephen wanted was to be back with Heidi. To see her for himself and know she was safe.

Could he sneak back down to Heidi while this guy was distracted?

Maybe. But it would be risky. His best bet would be to stay where he was.

However, that wasn't going to be possible for long.

He watched as the man walked toward the tracker. He paused in the area Stephen had left it. The man's foot moved along the ground, sweeping away some leaves.

Then he bent down and picked something up.

Stephen's lungs froze.

He'd found it.

Thank goodness they hadn't been on the other side of those rocks earlier or they would have been discovered. The thick granite had been the only thing stopping that signal.

What would this guy do now?

As the man glanced around, Stephen ducked back behind the tree.

His heart pounded in his ears. Had the guy seen him? He didn't think so, though he couldn't be certain.

Then the guy raised his radio and began speaking into it.

Stephen knew exactly what he was doing.

He was calling backup to this area so they could thoroughly search it.

Stephen couldn't let him do that.

CHAPTER
NINETEEN

STEPHEN DIDN'T WANT to use his gun. Only if he had to.

Instead, he grabbed a rock and threw it in the opposite direction.

As the man turned his head, Stephen darted from his location. He rounded some trees and approached the guy from behind.

Before the guy could realize he was there, Stephen launched forward and put the man in a headlock.

"What the . . ." The man thrashed against him, and his radio fell to the ground.

Stephen didn't think the guy had finished his call yet, that he'd given his location.

But he couldn't be sure.

The man continued to struggle against him, but Stephen was stronger.

He held him in the headlock for twenty seconds until the man went limp.

He wasn't dead, only passed out. But maybe this would give Stephen and Heidi just enough time to get away from here.

He grabbed the man's radio so he could hear any updates. Then he smashed the tracker in case anyone else could follow it.

Stephen darted back to where he'd left Heidi.

Her eyes were wide with fright when she saw him. When he saw the blood on her neck, it caused him to suck in his breath.

But she was okay. The blood was only from removing that tracker, he reminded himself.

He reached out his hand. "Come with me. We don't have any time to waste."

Her eyes were still wide as she nodded and scooted from her hiding place.

She took his hand, and the two of them began to run in the opposite direction.

There was no time to slow down. These guys weren't going to give up. That meant he needed to get Heidi out of here.

If someone was going through all this trouble to kill her, then she was definitely a valuable asset to whatever was going on.

Stephen had to keep her safe.

Not only for professional reasons, but because he had the undeniable urge to protect her. She didn't deserve any of this, and he'd do everything within his power to keep her safe.

———————

Heidi wished she could ask questions. But she couldn't.

All she could focus on right now was breathing and not losing her balance on the uneven terrain.

Whatever had happened back there had spurred Stephen into action.

If she had to guess, that man had found him.

She continued running, hardly able to catch her breath or catch up on her thoughts.

She did, however, notice the radio at Stephen's waist. He'd turned the volume low, probably because any noise from it would reveal their location. Had that radio belonged to one of their pursuers?

She didn't recognize it. It wasn't one of the ones Blackstone used.

Who were those men? Who had hired them?

Stephen gripped her hand, and they kept running farther down the mountain.

How far did this wilderness stretch? They could

probably walk for days out here without running into a road or anyone else, for that matter.

The thought made her shiver. She definitely wasn't equipped to survive in circumstances like this.

But she knew Stephen would help her.

She wasn't sure if she should be thankful for his presence or not. When he'd broken into her house, that was when everything had taken a shift.

They reached a stream and paused.

Heidi leaned forward, her hands on her thighs as she tried to catch her breath.

Finally, she glanced up. She saw a thin sheen of sweat spread across Stephen's face. Otherwise, he appeared unaffected by their swift escape.

"You doing okay?" He shifted to look her in the eye.

She nodded and used her sleeve to wipe the sweat from her face. "I suppose. But how much longer do we have to do this?"

"That's what I'm trying to figure out." He scanned their surroundings again as if making sure he wasn't being followed. Then he grabbed the radio from his waist and turned up the volume.

Voices crackled through the speaker.

"We found MacAvoy," the voice said. "Someone knocked him out."

"Then we must be close," another unfamiliar voice said in response.

"What do you want us to do?"

"Keep looking. They have to be around here somewhere."

A knot formed in Heidi's stomach. That wasn't what she wanted to hear. She wanted to hear that these guys had decided to give up. But she'd been hoping for too much.

The race for survival was still going strong, and she didn't have any time to recover. They needed to keep moving.

She glanced up at Stephen. "What about Gage?"

His jaw hardened. "I haven't heard from him."

"Do you think he's okay?"

"These guys didn't say anything on the radio." He held it up. "That's a good sign. Gage is capable."

"I know . . . but these men are dangerous."

Stephen didn't argue.

Instead, he held out his hand. "We need to keep moving."

She stared at his thick, strong fingers another moment before placing her hand into his again.

Then they continued their escape.

CHAPTER
TWENTY

STEPHEN AND HEIDI had been navigating the mountainous forest for three hours.

With each step, they disappeared deeper and deeper into the wilderness.

The sun was already beginning to sink, and soon it would be dark and cold outside.

The good news was that he hadn't heard any signs that those men were on their tail. Not yet.

But as the day drew on, Stephen sensed Heidi was growing exhausted. He had a feeling all she'd eaten today was that peanut butter sandwich at the house, and she hadn't even finished that. They were nearing the end of their limits and would need to stop soon.

They reached a heavily wooded area, and he paused. The trees would offer protection.

"Let's stop here a moment," he murmured.

Heidi leaned against a large oak tree and sucked in several deep breaths. Her cheeks were flushed with exertion.

As she caught her breath, he turned the radio on again. He couldn't afford to keep it on as they hiked. The sound of it would be a dead giveaway.

"We lost them," one of the men said, his voice staticky.

"What do you want us to do?" another guy said.

"We'll have to resume the search in the morning. Maybe get a plane out, if possible, and see if we can find them. We chased them deeper into the heart of the mountains. There's no way they're going to get out, especially not if we surround them."

Did these guys not realize that one of their radios was missing? Maybe they assumed it had fallen off a nearby cliff or something. They were certainly speaking freely.

Or maybe everything they said was a scam. Maybe these men were manipulating the conversation so Stephen and Heidi would think they were safe when they weren't.

Stephen needed to keep these things in mind to be on the safe side.

Clipping the radio back to his belt, he grabbed his phone. He frowned when he saw there was only one bar of service. Would that be enough for him to get in touch with Gage?

Calling him was risky, especially considering the chance his phone might ring.

Instead, he sent Gage a text message.

> Where are you? We're safe. But we
> need an escape plan.

He stared at the message, hoping he might get an instant reply.

He didn't. There was no indication the message had been read and no bubbles indicating Gage was responding.

Stephen prayed his friend was okay.

He put the phone away and glanced back at Heidi.

Apprehension showed in the knot between her eyes. But at least she wasn't breathing as heavily. Her cheeks weren't quite as red.

"Are we going to keep moving?" she asked.

He glanced around, his jaw tightening. "It's too dangerous. It's getting dark, and we don't know our way around this wilderness well enough. We should stop for the night and start again in the morning."

"From the sounds of it, these guys are going to keep looking for us."

"We'll start earlier than they do," Stephen said.

"Right now, we have an advantage because we have one of their radios. I'm not sure I want to trust everything they're saying, however. But right now, their conversation makes sense."

Heidi nodded before glancing around at the grove of trees surrounding them. "So we're staying here?"

"The trees will provide cover for the night. Plus, we're high enough that we have a small signal on my cell. I'm hoping to hear back from Gage so we can develop some type of plan."

"Even if we're able to get in touch with him, how would he get us out of these mountains? There are no roads. No rivers where a boat might even be able to pick us up. We have no food or water."

Stephen knew the situation was dire.

"I have a little water, but I'd like to save it. When that runs out, we can find a creek if we need. I have a protein bar in my backpack you can have. Otherwise, our bodies will survive without food for one night."

"I know that but . . ." A frown tugged at her lips. "To be honest, I'm scared."

He reached for her then rubbed her arm in an effort to offer some comfort. "It's okay to be scared. The circumstances we've found ourselves in right now are extraordinary."

"Extraordinarily bad you mean?"

He let out an airy chuckle. "Yes, I suppose that is what I mean."

"I don't like any of this. These guys are determined to kill us. Or to kill me. They don't even know you're with me, I suppose."

"They are determined. Someone wants you dead, and they'll do anything to make sure that happens."

"But it doesn't make sense why."

"Unless there's something you know that is worth killing you over. But what would that be?"

She raked a hand through her hair before shaking her head. "I wish I knew."

"We need to figure it out. Maybe it's something that seems innocuous. But whatever it is, it's a threat."

"A threat to who?"

Stephen frowned again. "That's also something that we have to figure out."

―――――

Heidi scooted closer to the fire.

She was amazed Stephen had been able to find enough pieces of dry wood to start a nice-sized fire. He told her the flames couldn't be too large, however. He didn't want to be spotted because of it.

However, the temperature had probably dropped down into the forties this evening.

She wasn't sure how the sleeping situation would work tonight. They had no blankets, and she had no jacket. Just the fire. She supposed she would be able to use her arm as a pillow and sleep close to the warm flames.

At least Stephen was here. He sat on the ground beside her, staring into the fire.

She was hungry, but she hadn't asked for that protein bar yet.

They could still be out in the woods all day tomorrow. If that was the case, she would need the food more then than she needed it now.

"How's your shoulder?" he asked.

She moved it, felt the tautness there. "It's okay. I'm just glad that tracker is gone."

His expression tightened. "Listen, Heidi. I'm sorry you've been pulled into the middle of this."

"It's not your fault. I'm the one who took this job." She let out a long sigh. "This all feels very surreal."

"Believe me, I never expected any of this either." He paused. "You know, I never told you this, but you're the reason I'm the person I am today."

She raised an eyebrow. "What do you mean?"

He let out a breath. "When we went to the office

for our debriefs, I saw a plaque you had hanging behind your desk. It said, 'Consider it pure joy, my brothers and sisters, whenever you face trials of many kinds, because you know that the testing of your faith produces perseverance. Let perseverance finish its work so that you may be mature and complete, not lacking anything.'"

"James 1:2–4. It's my favorite verse. It reminds me to be strong."

"I hadn't really thought much about Jesus or the Bible. But that verse made me curious. I went out, bought a Bible, and started reading it."

"That's great."

"It made sense to me. My neighbor was always leaving for church on Sunday mornings, so I started asking questions. My life changed after that."

"All that started from a little plaque I had hanging up, huh?"

He nodded. "It did."

She studied his strong profile. "How did you get involved with these people, Stephen? You seem better than this."

His jaw twitched as he stared at the fire. "As you probably remember, Rafferty tasked me with being one of Monarch's guards for personal protection."

"I do remember. That was right before you left

Blackstone." The whole thing had been confusing, and Rafferty hadn't offered any details, of course.

"Until that day, I was pretty much resigned that I'd do this for the rest of my life, that I'd work these jobs for Rafferty. I didn't really think much about it."

"What changed?"

"Nathan died."

She frowned at the memory. "But he died from sudden cardiac arrest."

Stephen's cheek twitched, and his voice was notably more stoic as he said, "That's what someone made it look like. But I don't buy it. I think someone killed him. That's what happens when people get too close to the truth. There were a number of warning signs I tried to ignore. But that became nearly impossible after a while."

"So that was it? You had suspicions about his death, so you quit?"

Stephen shook his head, the movement heavy with emotion—and maybe regret. "I met some other guys who were like me, only they worked for a different organization. They told me what they'd discovered about the trackers and heart implants. Then I learned Rafferty's background. Though I knew some of it beforehand, there was a lot he hadn't disclosed. That's when I knew without a doubt he was up to no good."

"So you just left?" She liked a man who was decisive and who had conviction.

"I didn't just leave. But we were in a situation where I had to pick sides. Rocky showed up."

Rocky Velasquez—who'd also gone by Alfie—had been another Blackstone operative.

"What happened to him?" Heidi asked. "Rafferty was tight-lipped about his disappearance."

"He disappeared around the same time the devices near our hearts were activated," Stephen said. "That was when I knew I had to figure out what was really going on. I had to put a stop to it, especially if there are guys out there willing to do whatever Rafferty tells them—no matter the cost."

"Most of the jobs we get seem pretty cut-and-dried," Heidi said.

"They do. But that doesn't mean there aren't things going on behind the scenes."

"I guess you're right."

Stephen turned to study her now, and she wondered what he was thinking. What kind of questions were on his mind.

She didn't ask. He'd bring them up when, and if, he wanted to.

Instead, he cleared his throat and looked away. "Enough about that for now. What about you, Heidi? Why did you take this job?"

"I'd been working as the administrative assistant for a CEO in Atlanta. I thought it was what I wanted to do until my mom was injured in a car accident and required around-the-clock care. Though insurance covered some expenses, it didn't cover everything. I didn't want to put her in a facility, so I began looking for a job where I could work at home and take care of her at the same time. That was five years ago."

"Did you see a job listing with Blackstone?"

"Actually, Rafferty approached me. He said he was looking for someone and that a headhunter had recommended me, even though I hadn't actually hired this headhunter. At the time, it seemed a little weird but not incredibly suspicious. I figured the headhunter must have seen my résumé posted online. I know things like that do happen sometimes, and I figured this person would probably get some type of payment from Rafferty."

"So he interviewed you after that?"

"He did. He seemed a little intimidating to be honest." The memory of that meeting flooded back to her. "I told him what had happened with my mom and that I was taking care of her. He wasn't bothered by that. Said it was honorable, actually. He offered to pay me a very nice annual salary and said I could work at home most of the time, that I'd only need to be in the office a few hours a week. The job offer felt like an answer to prayer."

Stephen narrowed his eyes as if annoyed. "Rafferty can be very convincing."

"He was. For a long time, he seemed like a decent boss. I mean, he wasn't always nice, and some of the assignments made me cringe. But I figured that was the nature of a private security firm."

He shifted in his seat. "Tell me about your mom— if you don't mind."

Heidi glanced at her hands as the memories flooded her. There was still a hole in her heart from her mom's absence in her life, and she knew there always would be.

The two of them had been close. They even looked alike.

They'd only had each other to rely on since Heidi's father had died of a heart attack before she was born. Her mom had always told her how much he would have loved her.

Her throat burned at the thought.

"She passed away last year," Heidi finally said.

"I thought I heard something about that." His voice softened. "But I was out on an assignment at the time. I didn't know how to bring it up to you the next time I saw you, but I am sorry."

"Thank you. It's weird when you give four years

of your life to taking care of someone full-time, and suddenly they're no longer there. That's not to mention the twenty-five other years that were spent with her taking care of me. I mean, I suppose after I went to college there was a little bit less of that. But a mother is always a mother. The role reversal was a bit jarring."

"I can only imagine."

She listened to the crackle of the fire for another moment. "I guess you didn't grow up with your parents?"

Stephen grabbed a stick and poked the fire. "No, like most of the guys in the program, my parents are out of the picture. Mine actually gave me up when I was less than a year old."

"So, you were adopted?" She wasn't sure why that fact surprised her, but it did.

She'd figured he'd probably been in foster care or placed in a children's home. Adoption could mean a loving home, which didn't fit what she knew about the guys at Blackstone.

"Yes, I was adopted by a very nice couple. When I was eleven they both got cancer within a year of each other and died. I was put into foster care for several months. Eventually, my adoptive mother's sister took me in. But we never really bonded. I'm not even sure why she ended up adopting me because she never seemed to want to be a mom. She pretty much just let me do my own thing."

"I'm sorry." She lowered her voice. "I know that must have been difficult."

"It was. But there's nothing I can do to change any of that. I just have to believe it made me into the person I am today."

"And it made you a perfect target for Rafferty." Heidi frowned as she said the words. But a surge of protectiveness rose in her.

"I suppose it did. But I'm ready for things to change."

She glanced up at him, her heart growing tender. "I can only imagine that's true."

"On more than one level," he murmured. "On more than one level."

CHAPTER
TWENTY-ONE

STEPHEN COULD HARDLY SLEEP. He listened to every sound, knowing he couldn't let down his guard, especially considering those guys were still out there.

For a while, he'd monitored the radio. But the guys on the other end must have gotten wise to it. They'd stopped communicating, and he hadn't heard anything for several hours.

He didn't like not knowing what was going on.

He'd also tried to contact Gage several more times, but none of his messages had gone through.

Stephen prayed his friend was okay. If he'd been captured, Stephen hadn't heard anything about it on the radio earlier.

As he lay there, he glanced across the fire to where Heidi was sleeping.

She looked almost angelic as her ringlet curls fell across her face. She seemed so different from him—but in a way that was fascinating. She was smart and wholesome. His upbringing and his job had made him hard. But around her . . . he felt like a better person.

She shivered on the ground, and his heart panged. He wished he had something to comfort her with, to keep her warm. He'd even love to pull her into his arms to keep her warm. But that would be inappropriate.

Still, a guy could dream.

But someone like Heidi would never want to be with someone like him. He was too rough around the edges. There were too many unknowns surrounding his past. What if something triggered him one day and he were to hurt her?

He'd never forgive himself.

No, Heidi deserved only the best.

Stephen wasn't the best. He was broken.

Finally, at five a.m., he rose.

It was still dark outside, but daylight wouldn't be their friend in this situation.

They needed to get moving and try to put more distance between themselves and the men chasing them.

Getting away would be treacherous, and Stephen prayed God would watch over them.

————

Heidi hadn't rested well, and she suspected Stephen hadn't either.

Her head was still full of cobwebs as she and Stephen got ready to start their day.

Stephen had grabbed a water bottle from his bag. "Drink some of this. You don't want to get dehydrated."

She took it from him and took a sip. The liquid felt refreshing, but her stomach rumbled. She was hungry. However, eating could wait. She'd rather get to safety first.

"How's your shoulder now?" Stephen asked. "Do you mind if I take a look?"

"Sure." She pulled her sweatshirt down and rolled her neck away to get her hair off the spot.

As Stephen's fingers moved over her skin, her blood raced. Why was she having this reaction? Why did her skin feel on fire?

And why, as Stephen leaned close, did she imagine what it would be like if he were to press his lips against her skin?

Inappropriate, she scolded herself. There would be no kissing.

Especially not with Stephen.

She needed someone with a stable job, with a background similar to hers.

At least, that's what she thought she needed.

"It looks good," he murmured. "No sign of infection."

"That's good news." But her voice cracked.

The sooner he stopped touching her bare shoulder, the better.

He released the collar of her sweatshirt, and it sprang back toward her neck.

She let out a breath.

"You ready to get moving?" Stephen asked.

"Ready as I'll ever be." She handed the bottle back to him, and he slipped it into his backpack.

He made sure the fire was extinguished and kicked dirt over it to try to hide the ashes.

A few minutes later, the two of them started walking away from the area where they'd slept.

Stephen kept a hand at her elbow as they traveled through the darkness. The trees looked skeletal with only the moonlight illuminating their branches. Occasionally, an owl hooted or dry leaves cracked under the weight of a small animal.

Rocks jutted into their path without notice, and they could only see a few feet in front of them.

Stephen reminded her several times to watch her step. That there could be cliffs or crevices anywhere, and he didn't know the terrain well enough to avoid the hazards.

"Were you ever a Boy Scout?" Heidi asked, using a sapling to keep her steady as the ground sloped downward.

He raised his eyebrows. "What?"

She shrugged, trying to keep her thoughts occupied and off the danger around them. "You seem like the type who would have been a Boy Scout."

He let out a soft chuckle. "Maybe in a different life I would have been."

"Did they teach you survival skills through Project Elevate? I can only assume that was the case." As her foot began to slip, Stephen gripped her arm more tightly, and she found her balance.

But her pulse kicked up a notch.

"They taught us pretty much everything," Stephen explained. "Languages. Survival skills. Every type of physical training you might be able to imagine."

"Sounds tough."

"It was, but the program weeded people out pretty quickly."

She glanced at his face in the darkness, wishing she could make out the fine details. "How did you even discover what was going on with Blackstone?"

"Nathan's sister came looking for answers." His voice turned grim. "The two of them had gone to separate homes while in foster care. I don't think when Nathan entered the program that the leaders knew exactly how determined Tori would be to find him. One thing led to another, and the truth became apparent. Only the truth wasn't exactly what I wanted it to be."

They walked a couple of moments in silence. Her thoughts raced. She wanted to know more about this man—beyond what she'd learned on the job. And he seemed open to talking, to sharing.

She skirted around another tree, grateful the ground was leveling out some. Soon, the sun should peek over the mountains.

"What about you, Heidi?" Stephen asked before she could question him more. "What do you do when you're not working for Rafferty?"

She let out a breath and shrugged. "It's going to sound lame, but I'm still trying to rediscover exactly who I am. For four years, every free moment I had was poured into taking care of my mom. I think I forgot about myself in the process. Since she's been gone . . . I've been trying to remember who I am."

"What kind of things did you like to do before your mom came to live with you?"

Her mind raced back in time. "I used to love traveling. Trying new restaurants. Chasing the sunset."

"Ever been married?" he asked, then hesitated. "That's probably too personal, isn't it?"

"Considering everything that's happened, I think we're way beyond the too-personal portion of getting to know each other." She flashed him a smile. "And, no, I've never been married. I was engaged once."

He hurried in front of her and offered his hand as they came to a small creek.

She carefully hopped on the large river rocks to get across.

"What happened—if you don't mind me asking?" Stephen dropped her hand.

She instantly missed it.

"Bryant liked to travel also," Heidi told him. "He wanted to live a more carefree lifestyle. When I had to take care of my mother, that put a real crimp in his plans. So he left."

"Ouch." He grimaced. "That couldn't have been easy."

She shrugged. "It wasn't. But it's better that I discovered his character before marriage rather than after. I mean, Bryant wasn't really a bad guy. At least, he was honest with me."

"That's one way of looking at it." Stephen twitched his head as if uncertain.

Heidi cast a glance at him. "What about you? Have you ever been married?"

"I guess it's only fair if I ask you that you can ask me also. But the answer is no. Never been married. I've dated some, but it's hard to maintain any kind of relationship with my schedule. This job is the type where it's easier just to be single, I suppose. I've been unattached for most of my life. It's what I'm used to."

She drew in a shaky breath as they started uphill. The air was thinner up here, and her lungs burned.

"I'm sure that's the way Rafferty wanted it," Heidi said. "He wants all his guys unattached, doesn't he? I noticed that about Blackstone soon after I started working there. That none of the guys were married or seemed to have a significant other in their lives. I just didn't understand the reasons. Now it's starting to make sense."

"It's a job where they want you to give every-thing, I guess you could say."

"I get that. Rafferty likes for me to be on call 24/7."

Just then, a sound cut through the air.

A chopping noise.

She and Stephen paused. The wind kicked up,

tugging at her hair as the sound became louder. When she looked up, she saw a light.

A helicopter, she realized.

Had the men who were chasing them tracked them down again?

CHAPTER
TWENTY-TWO

STEPHEN TUGGED Heidi under the branches of a tree before the spotlight hit them.

He didn't know who was aboard that helicopter, and they couldn't take any chances. With the darkness, it would be difficult to identify anyone.

"Stephen . . ." Heidi whispered as she clutched his arm.

It was almost impossible to hear her over the whomping of the helicopter blades.

If only he could get a better look at the aircraft itself . . . but it was too dark.

Just then, his phone dinged.

He glanced at the screen, and his pulse quickened.

It was Kai Kaleo, another colleague.

Stephen put the phone to his ear. "Kai?"

"Stephen, it's me," Kai said. "We're in the copter, looking for you. Can you see or hear us?"

Stephen turned to Heidi. "It's them. Some of my colleagues."

Heidi's eyes widened with hope. "Praise God!"

"Yes, we can see you," Stephen told Kai. "I'm going to turn on my flashlight so you can see where we are."

Stephen stepped out from beneath the tree branches and began to wave the light at the chopper.

Please . . . let them see us.

Instead, the copter headed farther away.

"Kai, do you see us?" he yelled into the phone.

When he didn't hear a response, he put it to his ear. "I think we lost our connection."

"We can't let them get away!" Heidi yelled.

They both waved, but the copter still headed away from them.

He dialed Kai's number again.

The call didn't go through.

His heart thudded.

"What are we going to do?" Heidi asked.

"Keep trying to get their attention." He cupped his hands around his mouth. "Over here!"

He knew he probably couldn't be heard over the helicopter's engine. But he tried anyway.

He waved his flashlight again and prayed—prayed hard.

I know I don't deserve this. I've done things I regret. Things I shouldn't be forgiven for. But help us. For Heidi's sake. She doesn't deserve this.

Just then, the aircraft swooped around. Headed back toward them.

Maybe the men onboard did see them after all.

But their problems weren't over yet.

Stephen glanced around as their next challenge hit him. "There's nowhere for them to land here. We need to find somewhere flat and cleared of trees."

"How much space do they need to land?"

"About a hundred square feet."

Heidi scanned everything around them. "I'm not sure we're going to find a clearing that big."

"Me neither. But we need to move."

Just then, a bullet split the air.

Stephen's breath caught.

Those men chasing them . . . they must have seen the helicopter hovering overhead.

Now they knew Stephen and Heidi's location.

He grabbed Heidi's hand.

Who would get to them first—his team in the helicopter or the gunmen?

————

Heidi instinctively ducked, even though she wasn't sure where the bullets were coming from. She thought the gunmen were aiming at the helicopter, but she couldn't be sure.

Either way, she needed cover.

"This way!" Stephen tugged her through the forest, moving so quickly her feet felt as if they only skimmed the ground.

Heidi hardly knew what was in front of her. Occasionally, a branch or a thick grove of trees or a boulder seemed to appear out of nowhere. Sometimes the ground was slick with leaves, and sometimes it was flat with dirt.

It didn't matter. They kept moving.

The helicopter hovered in the distance.

Seeing it was a comfort—help was here. But it was also a dead giveaway of their presence.

"Kai said there's a place in the distance where they can land," Stephen yelled over the noise of the copter as he glanced at his phone. "We just need to get to it in time."

"I feel like we're headed toward the gunmen."

When Stephen didn't answer, she knew what that meant.

They *were* headed toward the gunmen.

She prayed even harder. She hadn't stopped ever since they started this, to be honest.

They ran until her lungs burned and her muscles protested.

Then Stephen seemed to slam on brakes behind a cluster of trees.

She sucked in a sharp breath as she ducked around him to see why he'd stopped.

She saw the clearing ahead. Saw the helicopter landing.

How close were the gunmen?

"We don't have much time!" Stephen shouted. "We need to make a run for it. But stay low!"

As the copter got closer to the ground, Stephen's grip on her hand tightened. "Now!"

But just as they began to run, more gunfire exploded.

CHAPTER
TWENTY-THREE

STEPHEN PUSHED HEIDI BEHIND HIM, shielding her body with his.

They kept their heads low and their steps quick as they darted toward the helicopter.

The door opened, and Kai and Trevor leaned out. Working in tandem, they pulled Heidi inside as Stephen dove in.

The next second, the chopper was airborne again.

Kai worked fast getting Heidi secured as Trevor fired rounds back at their enemies.

Stephen jerked on his seatbelt as he glanced out. Four gunmen emerged from the woods, their rifles aimed at the copter.

His gut tightened.

This still wasn't over.

The pilot turned the helicopter away from the men.

Then he swooped into the air.

Trevor continued to fire back.

But Stephen didn't dare feel any relief yet. Too much was still at stake.

Bullets clanked against metal. Pinged against the cockpit and landing skids.

He waited for an explosion.

None came.

He waited for the copter to career out of control.

It didn't.

The bullets must not have hit the fuel line or damaged anything vital.

Praise God!

Several seconds later, they soared over the mountains. The sun peeked over the range in the distance, casting its warm glow onto the changing leaves.

Finally, Stephen sat back and pulled on his headset.

He glanced around. Heidi was pale but unharmed. The pilot sat in the front seat, a man Stephen didn't recognize. Gage also sat up front, and Trevor and Kai were in the third row.

He adjusted the microphone over his mouth. "Am I ever glad to see you guys."

"Glad you're okay too," Gage said.

"How'd you find us?" he asked.

"I traced your satellite phone. I lost mine some-where in the woods or I would have called."

"Makes sense."

Stephen stole a glance at Heidi. She looked shaken and tired but okay. Still out of sorts, so to speak, but she was alive and unharmed. That was the most he could ask for in this situation.

He couldn't wait for this bird to land. He needed to discuss with his teammates what had happened. The stakes kept rising, and eventually they'd hit a tipping point.

————

An hour later, Heidi glanced at the property where they landed.

She was fairly certain they'd headed north away from Georgia and toward Tennessee. The mountains —beautiful in the daylight—had remained beneath them for most of the trip.

Now they were on several acres of land that had been cleared. The property was surrounded by wooden fences and a sprawling white ranch-style house sat at the center. Heidi couldn't be certain, but she thought she spotted horse stables in the back near a pond with a small fishing pier.

Wherever they were, it was beautiful.

If only she were here to enjoy it.

Once the blades stopped spinning, Stephen helped her out and kept hold of her arm as they walked away from the copter. She was grateful for his support. She wasn't sure her legs would hold her she was still so shaken.

She stole a glance back at the helicopter. Bullet holes marred the sides. There was one precariously close to where she thought the fuel tank was located.

She shuddered.

That getaway had been entirely too close.

She swallowed hard, her throat burning as she glanced at Stephen. "Where are we?"

He nodded toward the home in the distance. "All my guys told me was that we were in Tennessee. That they'd brought us somewhere we'd be safe and can develop our next plan of action."

"Being safe sounds like a good start."

He cast her a soft grin. "I agree."

Gage motioned to them, and they followed him across the lawn. Stephen stayed beside her the whole time.

Several minutes later, they stepped into a meticu-lously decorated, luxurious farmhouse.

Whoever owned this clearly had a lot of money.

She didn't ask questions. Not yet at least.

They kept walking until they reached a massive living room with wooden beams across the ceiling, a soaring fireplace, and floor-to-ceiling windows.

The rest of the guys left her and Stephen in the room.

A man with white hair sat in a leather recliner near the fireplace with his feet propped up by the chair. Something about him seemed frail yet strong at the same time.

The fact that Stephen gasped beside her really made her curious.

Just who was this man?

CHAPTER
TWENTY-FOUR

STEPHEN COULDN'T STOP STARING at the man in front of him. He couldn't believe his eyes.

"Larchmont?" Stephen finally muttered. "I thought you were in the hospital?"

"They released me a couple of days ago." His voice sounded unusually weak, yet it still held an underlying level of confidence.

"I see," Stephen stated. "No one updated me."

"I didn't tell anyone," Larchmont said. "I needed some time to regroup first. Besides, there were many other things going on, so I figured we had time."

Stephen crossed his arms, not appreciating being left in the dark. It was true that he'd never directly worked for Larchmont. But he'd given up everything to help out his new colleagues with the Shadow Agency. The fact that Larchmont was now awake seemed like a courtesy someone should have mentioned.

He glanced around. "This your place? They told me you lived in Wyoming."

"I have more than one home. This is one of them."

A woman stepped out from another door. Stephen instantly recognized her.

Cynthia. The wife no one knew Larchmont even had.

She'd taken charge ever since Larchmont was placed in ICU.

But she hadn't said much. She'd told the guys she wanted to give her husband a few more days to wake up before disclosing any information or making any decisions.

It appeared this was the moment.

Stephen turned back to Larchmont. "What happened?"

Larchmont's face remained grim. "When Rafferty first came up with the idea of implanting devices in the soldiers, I told him it wasn't a good idea. But he was insistent, and no one stopped him."

Stephen remained stiff, still cautious about the man. "How does that equate to you having a pacemaker?"

"I told him to test it out on me first. So he did."

"But even after Rafferty went rogue, you kept the device in you?"

Larchmont's gaze darkened. "That's where things get weird. The truth is that I had surgery to remove it. Only the person who did the surgery must not have been telling the truth. Because I clearly still had the device implanted—I just didn't know it."

Stephen gave himself a few seconds to let that sink in.

"Who ordered the surgeon to leave the device in?" Heidi asked.

"I'm looking into that now." Larchmont's lip twitched as if he wasn't pleased with that development. "But this doctor seems to have disappeared. I have to wonder if Rafferty got to him. Blackmailed him or something."

"Go figure," Stephen muttered.

"You never had any follow-ups with other doctors who told you that the device was still there?" Heidi asked. "What about the battery? It would have needed to have been changed."

"I'm still trying to get all those answers."

"So you had no idea you were under Rafferty's thumb either?" Stephen asked.

Larchmont shook his head. "Unfortunately, I did not. I had to learn that lesson the hard way. It almost cost me my life."

Cynthia squeezed her husband's hand.

Stephen stared at both of them, still trying to put the pieces together.

He didn't trust Larchmont. He'd told too many lies. Kept too many secrets.

But he just might have the answers they needed also.

"Thank you for rescuing us," Stephen finally said. "We would have been goners if you hadn't let the team use your copter."

"Of course." Larchmont nodded slowly, his eyelids slightly droopy. "We would have gotten you sooner if we'd been able to locate you."

"What are we all doing here?" Heidi asked.

Larchmont's cheek twitched as he turned to her. "I'm glad you asked. I really need to speak with you, Heidi."

She pointed at herself, and surprise laced her voice as she asked, "You need to speak with me?"

"That's right. You might want to sit down, though. Because this won't be a fun conversation."

———

Heidi's mind was already spinning, and Larchmont hadn't told her anything yet.

Still, she lowered herself onto a nearby leather

couch, and Stephen sat beside her. On the coffee table in front of them were some crackers, cheese, nuts, and grapes, as well as a pitcher of water and two glasses.

Her stomach grumbled. But eating would have to wait.

She and Stephen turned toward the man, waiting for him to share his news.

"What I'm about to say isn't going to be easy to hear." Larchmont sounded weary as he said the words.

"I can handle it," Heidi assured him.

His cheek twitched again, almost as if whatever he had to say was painful for him also.

That fact put her on edge.

"Your mother was Theodora Myers," he started.

Heidi's back muscles instantly tightened at the mention of her mother. "That's right. Why are you bringing up my mom?"

"What did she tell you she did for a living?"

"She worked for a healthcare company in downtown Atlanta." Her mind raced as she wondered what he was getting at.

"The truth is, Heidi . . . your mom worked with Project Elevate."

Her eyebrows shot up. "What? No, that can't be right."

Larchmont nodded, no hints of deceit in his gaze. "Unfortunately, it's true. She had an alias, of course, because everybody who worked with the program did. We couldn't let people know what was really going on."

Heidi shook her head, unable to comprehend what he'd just said—or maybe she just didn't want to believe it. "She did *not* work for Project Elevate."

"But she did," Larchmont said. "She was Rafferty's assistant."

Heidi rubbed her temples, a sudden headache coming on. "That can't be right."

"I know this is hard to hear."

"Go on." Part of her didn't want to hear any more, but she knew she had no choice.

"She worked for Rafferty for many years. Then, when he started to become unhinged, she became wary. She quit, even though Rafferty expected her to stay. Honestly, I think he'd become quite fond of her, and I'm not just referring to professionally."

Heidi tensed. "Is that so?"

"When she started working for them, you weren't even born yet. Your father had died while your mom was pregnant."

"That sounds about right, from what I remember."

"So when she left the company, you were in your early twenties."

"Okay . . ." Heidi tried to be patient and figure out where he was going with this.

"That same year, your mom was in the accident that essentially left her in a vegetative state, correct?"

Bile churned in her stomach at the memories.

"That's right." Then she realized what Larchmont was hinting at. "Wait . . . you're telling me that *Rafferty* was behind her accident?"

Larchmont's face remained grim. "Yes, I believe that's true. I believe he tried to silence her because she knew too much. He never expected her to survive. However, since she was in a vegetative state, he no longer considered her a threat."

Heidi's muscles thrummed with tension. "So what are you getting at?"

Part of her knew the truth, but she didn't want to acknowledge it yet. She needed to hear the admission. Needed Larchmont to say the words out loud.

"You brought your mother home to live with you." He said the words slowly, carefully. "When that happened, Rafferty made sure to offer you a job that checked all your boxes."

"Why would he do that?" Her voice rose with frustration.

"So he could monitor the situation with your

mom. Just in case she ever started to speak again and tell you anything."

Heidi shook her head, her temples pounding even harder. "If that's true, and if my mom could understand anything going on during that time . . . then she would have known I was working for Rafferty. She wouldn't have been able to do anything about it. She was unable to speak, to communicate, but the doctor said she could still understand." Her voice cracked. "It would have been agony for her."

Compassion flooded Larchmont's eyes as he nodded. "I know. That's because he's heartless like that. The only person he truly cares about is himself."

"But . . ." Heidi didn't even know what else to say. Should she even believe this guy? He wasn't exactly the picture of virtue.

But her mother was no longer around to talk to either.

It reminded her again of the hole that had been left in her heart after her mom's passing.

Stephen softly placed his hand on her back, offering her a small measure of comfort.

However, it would take time to comprehend everything she'd just learned.

CHAPTER
TWENTY-FIVE

STEPHEN'S THROAT TIGHTENED.

He hadn't known any of this. Larchmont hadn't shared this information with him. He didn't even know if it was all true or not.

Either way, his heart panged with empathy for Heidi.

None of this could be easy to hear.

More than anything, he wanted to grab her hand and comfort her. But he couldn't do that. Especially not now. Not in front of Larchmont.

However, the grief on her face broke his heart.

"Why are you telling me this now?" Heidi stared at Larchmont, something close to contempt in her gaze.

"Because we need to find Rafferty and stop him."

"Stop him from doing what?" Her voice pitched

higher. "Haven't all the guys on your team had those devices removed from their hearts? Why else do you want to find him?"

"This is bigger than that." Cynthia spoke for the first time, her voice strong and confident.

Stephen bristled at her words. "How is it bigger?"

"The intel we've heard has led us to believe that Rafferty is planning an assassination," Cynthia said.

"An assassination?" Stephen almost wanted to laugh—not that the subject was a laughing matter. The words simply hadn't been what he expected to hear. "I need to know more. Who is the target of this assassination plot?"

Larchmont's gaze locked with his. "All we know is that it's a high-level political leader, someone whose death would rock the nation."

———

Heidi blinked several times, unsure if she'd heard everything correctly.

Larchmont's words were like something straight out of a book or a movie. But definitely not reality.

Her thoughts raced. She needed to know more—even though she wasn't sure what she could do. She was out of her league right now.

Before she could find her voice, Stephen spoke. "Why would you think that?"

Larchmont let out a long breath and rubbed a hand over his face, clearly exhausted. "Rafferty didn't start out bad. His intentions were good, actually. Along the way, he simply became disillusioned."

"Keep going," Heidi said.

"He's unhappy with the current state of our country. He sacrificed everything for the missions he was in charge of—he dedicated his whole life to the country. He did those things in order to build the United States into a nation he could be proud of."

"I would say he succeeded," Heidi said. "We're a stronger country because of the sacrifices our military has made for us, not just recently but throughout the years."

Larchmont's lips flickered downward. "Unfortunately, Rafferty didn't see it that way. When the people above him began to give orders he didn't agree with, he began to feel as if everything he did was in vain."

"Is that when he broke away from Project Elevate?" Stephen asked.

Larchmont nodded. "Yes. He was quite vocal about his displeasure. He was actually fired."

"And then?" Heidi asked.

"It's a rather long story, but to get straight to the point, new world alliances have been formed."

"What does that even mean?" Stephen's eyebrows furrowed. "I'm aware of the current state of the world, but how does that affect Rafferty and his work?"

"Many of his missions involved subterfuge." Larchmont's voice gained more strength as he shared this part of the story. "He developed super soldiers who would do the jobs no one else could be trusted with. People like you." He threw Stephen a pointed look.

Heidi glanced at Stephen and saw his lips press into a tight line. She could only imagine the things he'd had to do.

"This subtle espionage that turned countries against each other, all so certain agendas could be met," Larchmont continued. "But now new alliances have been formed, and all the suffering that Rafferty saw—the deaths—felt like they were for nothing."

Heidi's heart beat hard in her ears. Alliances meant everything when it came to world peace. Political leaders needed to trust each other. But sometimes those alliances had to be perfectly orchestrated.

In those cases, she could understand why Rafferty would think the sacrifices he'd made were for nothing.

"I can see where that's a terrible thing." Heidi crossed her arms. "I truly can. But I still don't understand how this equates to assassinating a political leader."

Larchmont grimaced before continuing. "According to the intel I've gathered, he wants to leverage the upcoming election and ensure the right people are in office."

"Rafferty really thinks he can do that?" Heidi asked. "I mean, it's a little more complicated than removing someone from the picture, isn't it?"

"It's *definitely* more complicated than that. He has a lot of very powerful people on his side, powerful people who can pull strings. If he makes it look as if the opposing party was behind the assassination, then he can build support for his own issues." Larchmont paused and shook his head.

"So how does this all tie in?" Stephen shifted in his seat. "We've been chasing a lot of leads. But I don't understand how everything connects."

"We believe Howard Monarch has been helping Rafferty, that Monarch is involved in this assassination attempt as well."

"What reason would he have to do that?" Heidi asked.

"Financial gain." Cynthia raised her eyebrows. "Power."

"What about Davis and Wagner?" Stephen asked. "Are they connected with this?"

"Davis and Wagner?" Heidi's mind raced. "Who are they?"

"Commander Davis is a former military leader with the Joint Chiefs of Staff," Stephen explained. "And Wagner is Senator Tom Wagner of Nebraska. We've been keeping an eye on them over the past few weeks."

"Longer than that, actually." Cynthia raised an eyebrow. "Things were going on behind the scenes before you came onboard with this."

"Is one of them the commander Monarch mentioned?" Heidi asked.

"Maybe. We've concluded that Davis and Wagner are both in on this, that they're involved somehow with this overthrow." Larchmont swallowed hard, his eyes drooping as if this conversation were wearing him out. But he didn't seem ready to stop yet either. "The mission we're about to undertake isn't one for the faint of heart. It could cost us everything. Absolutely everything."

Heidi let his words settle as she waited for Larchmont to continue.

CHAPTER
TWENTY-SIX

STEPHEN SET down the glass of water he'd begun to drink. Suddenly, hydration didn't seem as important. "So what are we going to do to stop this plan?"

"We believe these men are meeting to discuss things." Larchmont took a sip of his own water.

"Aren't they too smart to be seen together like that?" Heidi asked.

"They think they're untouchable," Larchmont said. "That's going to be one of their greatest downfalls."

"Where is this meeting?" Stephen asked.

"That's what we need to figure out." A new emotion crossed Larchmont's face, one Stephen couldn't read. He had a feeling that whatever Larchmont was about to say was something he wouldn't like.

He waited a few seconds for Larchmont to continue.

As soon as the man's gaze turned to Heidi, the bad feeling in Stephen's gut grew even stronger.

"That's where Heidi comes in," Larchmont said. "We need her to tell Rafferty that she was abducted but escaped. She needs to ask for his help. Then, once she's back in Rafferty's good graces, we need her to find out more information."

Stephen had a visceral reaction to his statement, and his muscles began to quiver. "That's a terrible idea. It's too dangerous. Absolutely not."

Larchmont turned to him. "I appreciate your opinion, but the decision isn't yours. It's Heidi's."

He swallowed his retort and turned toward Heidi, anxious to hear her refuse Larchmont's request—as anyone in their right mind would.

Larchmont's proposal was unthinkable.

Absolutely unthinkable.

———

Heidi swallowed hard as she let Larchmont's words sink in.

Rafferty had tried to kill her mom. Had hired

Heidi essentially to monitor the situation. Now he may have even sent his men to try to kill her.

Only she wasn't exactly sure that was true.

If it was, then why had other men who worked for Rafferty also been killed?

She'd need to put those pieces together eventually.

But right now, all she could think about was Larchmont's proposal.

That she go undercover in order to find out more information.

Information on something that could have consequences reaching far beyond her. Far beyond the people in this house. Far beyond one community even.

Consequences that could affect an entire country. That could shape ideological thoughts. That could ignite the already brewing conflicts in the world.

For some reason, Heidi knew she was the person best equipped to stop this.

The thought was daunting, to say the least.

She remembered Deuteronomy 31:6: *Be strong and courageous. Do not be afraid or terrified because of them, for the Lord your God goes with you; he will never leave you nor forsake you.*

Larchmont stared at her, waiting for her response.

Stephen sat beside her, his gaze also on her.

Tension crackled in the room.

Everyone was waiting to hear how she'd answer.

Finally, she swallowed hard. "I'll do it."

As soon as the words left her lips, Stephen snapped out of his daze. "That's a bad idea."

"It's the only way." Larchmont's tone contained a new sternness.

"There's got to be something else we can do," Stephen argued back.

"I'm afraid not—and we're almost out of time." Larchmont's expression remained stony.

"He'll kill her!" Stephen lurched forward as he said the words.

Heidi reached out and rested her hand on his back, trying to reassure him.

"We'll put safeguards in place," Larchmont responded. "It's Heidi's choice to make."

Their conversation went back and forth like machine gunfire. She could hardly get a word in.

They argued about her as though she wasn't sitting right beside them.

"Enough!" She sliced her hand through the air. "Stephen, this man attempted to kill my mom." Fire burned through her blood at that thought. "I want to do this. No, it's more than that. I *need* to do this. Not just for my mom . . . but for my country."

CHAPTER
TWENTY-SEVEN

STEPHEN COULDN'T BELIEVE those words had left Heidi's mouth. Yet, on the other hand, he *could* believe them.

She was trying to do the right thing. But he had to make her realize she wasn't equipped for this.

Although she was capable, she wasn't trained in how to handle these things.

There were other ways. They just needed to figure out what those ways were.

Stephen turned to Heidi, his gaze hard. "Can I talk to you for a minute?"

Surprise flooded her gaze. "Okay."

"Alone."

"Of course."

He stood and took her arm, leading her away from Larchmont and Cynthia.

As soon as they were in the hallway away from the living room, he turned to her. "Heidi, I know you want to do the right thing, but you've got to see where this isn't going to end well."

"I can do it. I can find out the information you guys need to know. I'm a decent actress. I fooled Beau when he came to the house, didn't I? I can do this also."

"It's not a matter of *if* you can do it. I know you're competent. But Rafferty is a snake. If he finds out what you're doing, he won't hesitate to kill you."

Stephen didn't miss the shudder that rippled through her.

Good. She needed to understand the stakes in this situation. She *should* be scared.

The next instant, Heidi raised her chin, a defiant look in her gaze. "It's a chance I have to take. I know it sounds crazy, but I'm in the best position to find out information."

His throat burned with emotion. "So many things could go wrong."

"I know. That's why I'll need to be careful."

"But Heidi . . ." Stephen swallowed hard as he stared at her.

She still looked like a wreck—they both did. Yet she had a glow about her, a gentle beauty that was rare.

He had to find the right words, even though he knew her mind was made up. He still wanted to believe there was a chance he could change it.

"Why do you care so much, Stephen?" Her soft voice cut through his thoughts.

He swallowed hard as he considered how to respond. "Because you're . . . you're my friend."

She stared at him, questions swirling in her gaze.

He swallowed hard again. He often prided himself on being fearless, yet when it came to talking about his emotions, he felt . . . anxious.

He hardly knew what to do with the feeling.

But he also knew better than to give up.

He decided to finish his thought. "Because you're my friend, but I'd like you to be even more one day."

She stared at him, her expression unreadable.

Not exactly what he wanted. He'd hoped to see her face light up with agreement.

He'd hoped to realize the risk he'd taken was worth it.

Instead of smiling, she raised her chin. "Part of me wanted to hear that more than anything. But . . ."

"But what?" He hardly wanted to ask the question.

"I need to be with someone who lets me be my own person."

"You don't think I'd be that way?" He had no idea what she was getting at.

"I need to be with someone who will be with me through the thick and the thin. Who will respect my choices, even when they don't agree."

Stephen heard the emotion in her voice. Heard the hurt from her past relationship with Bryant. When she hadn't acted the way he wanted, he'd left.

Stephen knew how this looked. Knew it appeared as if he was trying to control her or give her ultimatums. *Be who I want you to be or else.*

But it wasn't like that. He only wanted what was best for her. She didn't have enough experience to see just how dire this was.

Before he could explain himself, Heidi took a step back. "I need to get some water."

"Heidi—" he started again.

But she kept walking, making no effort to hear him out.

———

Heidi closed the door to the bathroom and locked it, needing a moment alone.

She wasn't sure why she felt so angry. It wasn't because Stephen cared about her.

In fact, hearing his confession sent a small thrill

through her. If she were honest, she was beginning to care about him too. When she'd drifted to sleep last night, she'd even been thinking about what it would be like if she and Stephen were more than colleagues.

Their conversation reminded her too much of the talks she and Bryant used to have.

He'd always tried to convince her to see things his way. His ideas were the only ones that mattered. If she didn't go along, he'd become angry. Resentful. Sometimes even vindictive.

When the going had gotten tough, Bryant had left. Settled for an easy relationship without the complications brought on by Heidi's mother's accident and subsequent medical issues.

Heidi needed the freedom to be her own person and make her own decisions.

Right now, above all else, she had to do the right thing—even if it cost her everything.

How could she live with herself knowing she had the potential of stopping something horrible from happening to this country, but that she hadn't done everything in her power to do so?

She couldn't.

Even if she was terrified.

Heidi stared at the mirror, noting how rundown she looked right now. Her hair hadn't been washed in days, and now frizzy curls sprang out from her face. The wind from the helicopter had only made it look crazier.

Circles hung under her eyes, and a smudge of dirt stretched across her cheek. The dark blue of her sweatshirt concealed any blood from the emergency surgery on her shoulder. She knew that beneath her clothing there would be dried blood.

She cupped her hands and splashed water on her face. Took another sip of water.

Then she wiped her hands dry. Patted her face with a towel. Ran her fingers through her tangled hair.

This wasn't exactly the way she liked to present herself.

None of that mattered anymore. There were much larger issues she needed to deal with.

She drew in a deep breath before opening the door.

Now she needed to go talk to Larchmont about the first step of the plan.

She couldn't let Stephen stop her, even if his concern came from a good place.

She had to do the right thing, no matter what.

CHAPTER
TWENTY-EIGHT

STEPHEN TRIED to keep his frustration under wraps, but it was difficult—especially since Heidi would be stepping into danger. He couldn't stop her, and he knew that. However, Larchmont shouldn't have put her in this position.

Now it was too late.

Heidi had left the bathroom and avoided eye contact with him. She didn't want to talk, and Stephen wanted to respect that. Hopefully later she'd see things differently. Because he needed to clarify what he'd said.

That conversation hadn't gone as he'd planned. Not at all.

She'd gone back to meet with Larchmont and Cynthia. Larchmont was clearly exhausted and needed rest after everything he'd been through. But the man was determined to see this through. He'd said he could rest later.

As Heidi had addressed Larchmont, Stephen had hoped to hear that she'd changed her mind.

She hadn't.

Stephen and Gage had positioned themselves near the door while Heidi and Larchmont planned all the details. For the past two hours, they'd been rehearsing her cover story.

Stephen couldn't listen to this anymore. He needed a break.

As he excused himself and stepped out of the room, someone stepped out behind him.

"Hey, man." Gage's perceptive eyes met his. "I know this is a stressful situation. Are you doing okay?"

Stephen shook his head. "Not really. I hate this. I hate all of it."

"I know you do. But we're going to make sure Heidi is ready before we send her out there."

Gage sounded so certain. Stephen wanted to believe him. But this whole setup was dangerous. Too much could go wrong.

"I have a bad feeling about all this," he finally said.

"We'll be there to have her back," Gage assured him. "All the safeguards will be in place."

Stephen leaned against the wall. "I know. I appreciate that. But Heidi is still walking right into the lions' den. She has no training and no way to protect herself if things go wrong. If Rafferty catches wind of the fact she's deceiving him, she's a goner. Before we can get to her, he'll pull the trigger, and all this will be over."

Gage placed his hand on Stephen's shoulder, looking ready to talk Stephen down from the ledge. "I know this is hard. We just need to trust the process."

Trust the process? That would be easier said than done.

Especially since Heidi's life was on the line. She deserved better than this.

Why couldn't he be the one in this position? What he wouldn't give to trade places with her . . .

Stephen hated the helpless feeling brewing inside him, and he wished he'd never pulled Heidi into this. If anything happened to her, it would be his fault, and no one would convince him otherwise.

————

Heidi tried not to second-guess herself as she reviewed everything with Larchmont.

In between memorizing her cover story, she

munched on a sandwich someone had brought out for her. She was hungrier than she'd thought, and the turkey and cheese on wheat hit the spot.

The snacks that had been set out on the table earlier had already been devoured, not just by her but also by Stephen and Gage.

As they talked, she could tell Larchmont was getting tired. But he refused to give up. For that reason, neither did she.

She found the man's perseverance inspiring. But she also knew this was important to him. The situation was serious.

Stephen and Gage stepped back into the room, and she glanced at them. Stephen still looked uptight with his squared shoulders and heavy gaze. He didn't make eye contact—probably on purpose.

Maybe it was better that way. She didn't want to see the disappointment in his gaze.

His worry came from a good place. But she couldn't deal with those complications right now.

Maybe later. If she survived to see later.

She swallowed hard at the thought.

She finished reciting her cover story again and then waited for Larchmont's critique.

He stared at her a moment and then nodded. "Good job. Do you have any questions?"

She let out the breath she'd been holding. Then

she put her sandwich onto the paper plate on the table, only a couple of bites remaining.

What was she missing right now?

"How am I going to communicate with you guys?" she asked.

"Great question. At first, we were going to put a listening device in your earrings—"

"Rafferty would notice the new earrings and get suspicious." She wasn't the type to wear a lot of jewelry anyway.

"That's what we concluded as well. Instead, we came up with this." Larchmont motioned to someone in the distance.

A man Heidi hadn't seen before stepped inside. He carried a pair of shoes with him—shoes that looked an awful lot like the thick-soled running shoes she had on now.

It took her a few seconds to realize what Larchmont had done. "You put a listening device in those shoes?"

"It's more than that." Cynthia took the shoes from the man and showed them to Heidi. "The shoes actually have a special compartment in the sole."

Cynthia pressed a hidden lever on the bottom of the right shoe, and the sole pivoted. Inside the foam, nestled in the depths, was a small cell phone.

Heidi raised her eyebrows. "I have to admit . . . I'm impressed."

"If anything goes south, you can use the phone to call us," Cynthia said. "It should stay charged for a couple of days. We can also track you through the phone and listen to you."

"That's pretty amazing." Heidi stared at the shoe, feeling as if she'd stepped into an alternate reality. "I guess I just need to remind myself not to take my shoes off."

"Yes, by all means, see if you can keep wearing them, even if it means coming up with an excuse about why." Larchmont sat up. "Maybe it's that you're cold or your heels hurt or whatever."

She rubbed her temples as she tried to keep everything straight. "I feel like this is *Mission Impossible*—only it's real life."

Larchmont leaned closer, his weary eyes on her. "You can do this, Heidi. We'll be tracking your every move and listening to everything you say. We'll station people nearby, and if anything starts to go wrong, we'll move in. If you feel threatened at any time, we're going to give you a code word. You just say that word out loud, and we'll step in to help."

That was comforting, she supposed. "What's that code word?"

"Overwhelmed," Larchmont said. "It's a word

you should be able to easily work into the conversation if needed. When we hear that, we'll know to act."

She drew in a deep breath and nodded, trying to keep her composure and not freak out as the reality of what she was doing hit her. If she screwed up even just a little . . . this whole operation would be blown.

And she'd be killed.

She pressed her eyes closed, trying not to think about that.

Heidi forced her eyes open and looked at Larchmont. "So, when I get there, you want me to ask Rafferty questions, correct?"

"Yes, and if he doesn't answer those questions, then I need you to eavesdrop. Look in his office." Larchmont paused and locked gazes with her. "But whatever you do, don't get caught."

Don't get caught . . . that was going to be easier said than done. But her only choice was to succeed. Anything else would end in death.

Her death.

CHAPTER
TWENTY-NINE

STEPHEN STILL HATED everything about this. But the situation was out of his control.

At a pause in the conversation, he turned toward Larchmont. "I want to go with her when she's dropped off. I want to be in the vehicle that tails her. I want to be close in case things go south."

Larchmont observed him a moment before nodding. "As long as you don't get in the way."

"I won't," he promised.

They would drop Heidi off in the closest town. When she got there, she'd find a phone—either at a local business or she could borrow one—and call Rafferty. She'd tell him about her abduction and how she'd gotten away.

They'd already gone through the story several times.

But Stephen knew that in an ideal situation, an undercover operative should live with their cover story a while longer so the details felt more natural. However, in this circumstance, there was no time.

That didn't make him feel any better.

As Heidi excused herself and brushed past him without making eye contact, Stephen stepped closer to Larchmont.

Larchmont glanced up at him, his gaze weary as he seemed to read Stephen's thoughts. "She's got this."

He decided not to mince his words. "She's just a pawn to you, a player in the game. Someone who helps you get what you want."

"That's not true. I wouldn't ask her to do this if so much wasn't at stake."

Stephen leveled his gaze with Larchmont. "If she dies, her blood is on your hands."

Larchmont didn't miss a beat as he said, "If she dies, then we will all have blood on our hands."

———

Heidi was quiet on the drive to Norton. Larchmont believed Rafferty had stationed himself not far from the town. The place was close enough that he could go into Atlanta as needed but far enough away that he would have privacy.

That sounded like Rafferty.

As they drove, the sky became cloudy, and drizzle fell. It seemed appropriate considering the task before her.

She mentally rehearsed her cover story: Donald had been killed. The men who'd run them off the road had grabbed her. Taken her to a cabin in the mountains.

She'd managed to escape and had run until she could find help. But she feared those men were still after her.

There was enough truth in the story that she should be able to sell it.

However, if Rafferty was the one who'd sent those men after her, then he'd know she was lying. It was a chance she'd have to take.

As Heidi thought through it all, she glanced at her hands in her lap. Smudges of dirt still stained them.

Larchmont had instructed her not to clean up. She still needed to look bedraggled and dirty, like she'd been abducted and escaped. Her shoulder wound had been cleaned up, however. They didn't want Rafferty to know the tracker had been removed, even though he probably already did.

They'd even taken her new shoes and made them look dirty, caking mud on the soles.

Stephen was quiet in front of her as they drove. She could only imagine what he was thinking.

He'd made it clear he didn't approve of her going on this mission. But what choice did she have? She could do this. She *had* to do this. Too much was at stake.

Every time she thought about how Rafferty may have been the cause of her mother's accident, more anger and determination rose in her. Her mother deserved justice. Heidi would find that justice for her mother, if no one else.

Up ahead, she spotted a narrow main street. From what she'd heard Gage saying, fewer than a thousand people lived in what had once been a thriving coal-mining town.

Before they reached the historic business district, Gage pulled the SUV to the side of the road near a wooded area—far enough away that no one should see her.

The plan was to make it look as if she'd run from the woods and into town.

Gage craned his neck to look at her in the back seat. "This is it. You can do this."

Heidi nodded, though she felt anything but confident. "I'm ready."

In so many ways, she *was* ready. But that didn't mean she wasn't nervous.

She opened the door and cast Gage and Stephen one last look. Stephen stared at her but still said nothing. His eyes remained icy and cool—and unapproving.

She wished Stephen would say *something* to her. That he wasn't so angry.

He had to understand her motivation for doing this.

But his expression offered nothing.

He was upset, and she couldn't blame him. But she hated to end things this way.

She pulled her gaze away from him and stepped onto the grass on the side of the road. It was still gloomy outside, so no one was around. That was good. She couldn't afford to be seen being dropped off.

Now, she'd be on her own. This mission was up to her.

A tremble of nerves raked through her.

Just as she stepped away from the SUV, a shadow appeared beside her.

Had she already been spotted? She sucked in a breath, realizing how on edge she was.

She looked up, and Stephen stood there. His gaze

still looked tumultuous and his muscles tight as he stared at her.

Her heart leapt into her throat at the sight of him.

"Hey." His voice sounded hoarse. "Be careful, okay?"

She nodded stiffly, forcing the action. "I will be."

His concern filled her with warmth. It had been a long time since anyone truly cared about her. She'd been flying solo since her mom's accident.

She'd forgotten about how nice it felt to have someone watching out for her.

As she glanced at Stephen, she remembered his earlier words.

About being more than friends. The idea was intriguing.

In such a short time, their bond had grown strong. She'd come to depend on him. To care what he thought. To look forward to the time she had with him.

Her earlier reaction . . . it had been borne out of the urge to protect her heart. But if she didn't survive this, she didn't want that to be her last conversation with Stephen.

"Heidi . . ." he started.

"Don't," she told him.

"Don't what?"

"Don't say it."

"You don't know what I was going to say," Stephen murmured.

On a whim, she reached on her tiptoes and brushed her lips across his cheek. Electricity zapped through her, and she wanted to hover close. To linger near him for longer and absorb his warmth, his subtle evergreen scent, his burly strength.

But not in these circumstances, she realized. She had to be wise.

Instead, she stepped back, emotion clogging her throat. Surprise stretched through Stephen's gaze.

"You're going to get through this," he told her softly.

"I will." She forced a smile. "And when I do, we can talk about things."

"I'm going to hold you to that."

If she continued their conversation any longer, she might lose it. Change her mind. Jump into that SUV.

Instead, she turned on her heel.

Before she lost her courage, she jogged across the street to look for a phone.

She had to sell this. Her life depended on it.

CHAPTER
THIRTY

HEIDI WANDERED down the cracked sidewalk of the town time had forgotten.

She hadn't crossed paths with anyone—which didn't surprise her.

Instead, she scanned the various storefronts—an old restaurant, a furniture store, a general mercantile. But most of those places looked abandoned.

The pawn shop on the corner of town seemed her best option. She'd just seen a man leave the business and walk in the opposite direction, so the place must be open.

Here goes nothing.

She released some of the control she tried to exert over her emotions and instead let her trembles emerge. The tremors were real, and there was no need to hide them anymore. They'd only help sell her cover story.

She jogged toward the pawn shop, flung the door open, and tumbled inside. "Please . . . I need help."

A man in his sixties with frizzy, white hair and a pot belly rushed around the counter toward her. "Are you okay, ma'am?"

She knelt on the gritty carpet. "I . . . I need to use a phone. It's urgent. Please."

"Of course. You can use mine." The man paused. "Do you want me to call the police?"

"No!" she said sharply before softening her voice. "I have someone who can pick me up. I just need to call him. I don't want other people to get involved. It's . . . it's complicated."

"Of course." He grabbed a phone from behind the counter and handed it to her.

She pushed herself up to her feet and dialed Rafferty's number. Only a few people had his direct line, and she prayed he answered so she wouldn't have to put up this current act much longer.

"Who is this?" a deep voice barked a few seconds later.

Relief washed through her. "Rafferty . . . it's me. Heidi."

"Heidi?" His voice softened. "I've been trying to find you. I didn't know what happened."

"Donald . . ." As the man's image filled her mind, so did the thought of him dying. A cry lodged in her throat, one that was totally authentic. "We were run off the road. He died. Then some men grabbed me."

"What?" His voice rose. "Who?"

She glanced at the pawn shop employee and saw him listening. She needed to be careful what she shared. Otherwise, he really might call the police, which could ruin their whole plan.

"I don't know who they were," Heidi said. "I managed to get away. But now I don't know what to do. I need your help. Please."

"Where are you?"

"I'm in Tennessee, I think." She looked at the pawn shop employee. "What's the name of this town?"

He rattled it off.

"I'm at a pawn shop in Norton." Desperation cracked her voice. "Can you pick me up?"

"I'll send my men. It might take a while, but I'll have them there to get you. Okay?"

"Yes. Yes . . . thank you."

"Just stay where you are."

"I will." Heidi ended the call, deleted the number she'd just dialed from the recent calls, and thanked the man for letting her use the phone.

He stared at her, his shaggy eyebrows knit

together with concern. "Are you sure I can't call the police for you?"

That was the last thing she wanted. "No, I'll be fine. Believe me. It's better this way—it's better for you too. You don't want to mess with these people."

Fear flashed in his gaze, and he nodded. "Got it."

Using her thumb, she pointed over her shoulder. "I'm just going to wait outside for my ride. But thank you so much for your help."

"Of course."

"Please . . . forget you ever saw me. For both of our sakes." Then Heidi stepped outside.

This just might be the longest wait of her life.

It gave her too much time to think. To question herself. To doubt her decisions.

But she could do this. She could pull off this charade.

She glanced across the town to a street in the distance. Stephen and Gage's SUV was parked there.

She knew they were watching, which *did* make her feel better. But she also knew that once Rafferty picked her up, she'd be on her own.

Unless she cried *overwhelmed*. She hoped it didn't come down to that. She was the best chance they had for finding out the information they needed. She didn't want to blow this.

Finally, more than two hours later, a black van squealed to a stop in front of her.

Her heart thumped harder as she stared at the vehicle.

Were these Rafferty's guys? Or were these the people who'd killed Donald and Beau? Were those people one and the same?

She froze at the thought.

How could she be sure?

Before she had time to figure it out, the door slid open.

Two men she'd never seen jumped out. Grabbed her arms. Threw her in the van.

Her elbow hit the floor, and pain climbed through her arm.

But she didn't have time to think about her discomfort.

The door slammed shut.

Tires squealed as they accelerated from the pawn shop, headed . . . headed who knows where.

Their plan had worked. So far, so good.

But now would come the toughest part.

———

Stephen tensed as he stared at the van.

The vehicle blocked his view of Heidi. Blocked his view of seeing what was happening.

Then it had taken off.

With Heidi in it.

"Hey, what are you doing?" Heidi's voice came through the speakers on his laptop. "Ouch! You're hurting me."

Stephen's hands fisted. He wanted to jump out of the SUV. To find her. To pull her away from those men.

But it was too late. The plan had been set in motion.

Rafferty's men—whoever these new guys were—had her. Stephen had a feeling these were the guys who'd flunked out of Project Elevate. Larchmont had suspicions that Rafferty had kept them close at hand, just in case.

Most of them had failed because they'd been loose cannons.

That made them even more dangerous now.

He knew what these people were capable of, and he couldn't stomach the thought.

"When I asked Rafferty to have someone pick me up, I didn't mean I wanted someone to manhandle me," Heidi complained.

"Shut up. This isn't a time for conversation. This is an extraction."

Extraction? Maybe those guys really were with Rafferty.

Stephen wasn't sure if that made him feel better or not.

"Where are we going?" Heidi's voice sounded thin with fear.

"It's not important," the man said. "Now sit back. This isn't a therapy session. I don't want to talk."

Stephen fisted his hands. He didn't like the way this guy was speaking to Heidi.

"She's okay," Gage told him. "Just take a deep breath. Getting angry won't get us anywhere."

Gage was right. Stephen breathed in and out, trying to douse the fire flaring to life inside him. He had to stay focused.

He glanced at the laptop in his lap, at the beacon indicating Heidi's location.

In a few minutes, he and Gage would follow behind the van. They needed to be careful not to be spotted and blow this operation.

Heidi's life depended on it.

CHAPTER
THIRTY-ONE

"WHY CAN'T you at least tell me where we're going?" Heidi asked as she stared at the three strange men around her.

She'd expected to see someone she recognized. After all, she'd worked with most of the men Rafferty had hired.

At least, she *thought* she had—other than the three new hires. But apparently, that wasn't the case.

These guys had thrown her in the back of the van and then shoved her into a seat. One man sat beside her, and the other two were up front.

However, the van looked clean and respectable.

On second thought, maybe that wasn't a good thing. Maybe that meant these men were professionals who knew exactly what they were doing.

That could make this situation more precarious. She wasn't sure yet how she felt.

At least, they hadn't tied her up.

Yet.

"Aren't you going to answer me?" Her gaze shifted to each person in the van. "Where are you taking me?"

"I told you, stop asking questions," the man beside her barked. The guy was tall and thick, with a full head of dark hair and hard eyes. She'd never seen him before.

"Lay off, Edward," the driver muttered.

Edward. She had a name.

"I'm just scared." She rubbed her elbow, which still throbbed and had a touch of carpet burn. "You can't blame me for that."

"Like I said, where we're going isn't important. The best thing you can do is to be quiet."

Being quiet wouldn't help her find out the information she needed. "I need to see Rafferty. You're taking me to him, aren't you?"

Edward's eyes narrowed in annoyance. "Only Rafferty can make that decision."

She glanced at each of the men again. This was her time to find out information and relay it back to Stephen and Gage. She had to make the most of this opportunity.

She only wished they could talk to her. But they couldn't.

They'd thought having her wear an earpiece was too risky.

"Who are you guys even?" she asked.

"I've said this before, and I'm going to say it one more time," Edward grumbled. "You're asking too many questions. Be quiet—or I'll have to make sure you're quiet, and trust me, you don't want that."

Heidi clamped her mouth shut. Maybe this *wasn't* the time to find out more information. She'd be no good to anyone if she was dead. She'd pushed too hard.

Instead, she watched out the window as they left the small town behind and headed farther into the mountains, farther away from Stephen and Gage.

Even though they were tracking her, that fact didn't help quell her nerves right now.

She had to get this right, or she would pay with her life.

————

For the next hour and a half, Stephen continued to watch the screen as they followed the van, staying a safe distance behind to ensure they weren't spotted.

So far, so good—relatively speaking.

He hated everything about this situation, but at least this assignment hadn't gone off the rails yet. He prayed it wouldn't.

He stared at the screen and called out directions, trying to keep his calm.

And he did—until the dot on the screen stopped blinking.

He sat up straighter and sucked in a breath. The tracker had stopped in the middle of nowhere.

He jiggled the mouse, hoping it would become active again.

It didn't.

"What's going on?" Gage craned his neck toward him.

"The signal just stopped. It's not my computer messing up. Something went wrong."

"Maybe it will come back online. Maybe we just lost connection."

Stephen hoped that might be the case, but in his gut, he knew it wasn't.

He wasn't sure where these guys were taking Heidi. No one really knew anything about Rafferty and his personal life. The man simply doled out instructions while keeping a low profile.

Just then, the signal began working again, and Heidi's voice came through the speaker. "Where are we? What is this place? You're telling me that

Rafferty told you to bring me to an old, rundown shack that looks like a strong wind could blow it over?"

Relief washed over him. Good. She was okay— for now.

"You'll see," the man grumbled. "Now get out."

Stephen's heart pounded harder as he tried to picture the scene—this shack that she'd mentioned. He wished he could see what Heidi was seeing. But he couldn't. He only had her conversation to rely on.

"Ouch!" Heidi's voice sounded through the speakers on his laptop. "Stop hurting me."

"Then move."

"I *am* moving. You don't have to be a jerk."

Stephen bristled. If that man hurt her . . . he'd see to himself that the guy paid.

"I don't want to go in there." Tension rose in her voice. "Please. No!"

Then the feed went dead. Nothing but silence rang out.

"What the . . . ?" Stephen muttered as he adjusted the volume, hoping this was a fluke.

"They must have some type of signal blocker." Gage gripped the steering wheel harder. "At least we have her location."

"But we won't be able to hear if anything goes wrong," Stephen muttered.

This was exactly what he'd feared. That something wouldn't go according to plan. Nothing was ever simple with Rafferty.

He'd seen this coming, but no one had listened to him. Heidi would be the one who ultimately suffered because of that.

"Just hold tight and trust her." Gage kept his voice even and steady, no signs of anxiety. "Heidi has a good head on her shoulders. She can hold her own."

Stephen agreed with that assessment. But that didn't help him feel any better.

"We need to get to her location." Stephen's jaw hardened at his words. "We need to get there now."

CHAPTER
THIRTY-TWO

HEIDI TRIED to shrug out of Edward's grasp. He gripped her arm so tight that it hurt, but he didn't seem to care.

They'd driven down mountain roads, surrounded by nothing but woods before stopping at a shack surrounded by an open field. A weathered barn with a partially collapsed roof stood in the distance. Otherwise, there was nothing.

Why had these guys brought her here? The location didn't make any sense.

Unless these men planned on shooting her and leaving her where no one would find her.

Fear seemed to wrap its invisible fingers around her throat and squeeze, making it impossible to breathe.

Edward dragged her inside the shack.

"Why are we going in here?" she muttered, digging in her heels as worst-case scenarios played out in her head.

"Shut up," Edward muttered. "You're seriously giving me a headache. I have no idea why Rafferty likes you so much."

Rafferty liked her? That was news. However, he had handpicked her for the job. Was that because of her mother?

A musty scent hit her inside the shack. The floor was nothing but earth. Some old wooden furniture had been piled in corners.

What was going on?

Then Edward reached down. Tugged something on the ground.

She gasped when a door opened. This place was just a cover.

Edward led her downstairs. Through a long, dark hallway.

Creepy lights flickered overhead, and the place smelled dank, like earth.

At the bottom of the stairway, they reached another door. Edward punched in a code before ushering her inside a new area, this one more updated and less rustic, with an almost space-age efficiency.

The walls were metal and sterile. Tubes of

buzzing fluorescent lights ran neatly along the ceiling. Digital boxes bulged in front of each door, a keypad lit in red on the front.

Heidi's heart pounded harder as she realized where she was. A high-tech bunker, the perfect place for a criminal mastermind to plan his evil deeds.

And also a place no one would ever find her.

Even though Stephen and Gage were tracking her, a bad feeling brewed inside her. Could they even get a signal from her while she was underground?

"What is this place?" She needed to get more information.

Edward scowled. "All you need to know is what you see."

"I'm not the enemy here," she muttered.

"You might as well be."

Her heart thumped harder. She clearly hadn't won this guy over.

"What's it going to hurt to tell me what this is?" she continued to push.

Edward sighed. "We call it the Hive. This is where all the operations are based out of."

"Who built it? How does a place like this even come to exist?"

He continued to lead her down the hall. "When you have the right resources, you can do anything. But, if you must know, this was originally intended to be a bunker for political leaders in case of a nuclear fallout until the government decided to build a place in West Virginia instead. We just took the shell of this place and enhanced it, made it everything we needed. Then we built the shack and the barn to camouflage the space."

"Sounds very sci-fi-ish."

"Call it whatever you want."

She wondered how he fit with Project Elevate. Had he gone through the program with Stephen? Was he in a separate group, maybe one Stephen didn't know about?

Edward paused at a door and punched in a code on a keypad. After a beep sounded, he opened a metal door and shoved her into a room.

She caught herself before stumbling to her knees. As she straightened, she looked up and sucked in a breath.

Rafferty sat behind a metal desk, appearing as if he'd been waiting for her.

"You don't have to be so rough with her," he muttered to Edward. "What did I tell you?"

"She's mouthy and asks too many questions."

"Disobey me again, and I'll have some questions to ask you. Understand?"

Edward shifted behind her. "Understood."

Heidi rose to her full height and observed

Rafferty a moment. It had been several weeks since she'd seen him in person, and his looks had changed.

The man had a medium height and build. His hair was dyed jet black, and his face was pale, giving him an almost vampire vibe. His eyes, usually brown, were now green. Contacts? Maybe. Though he was probably in his early seventies, his skin was unnaturally tight, evidence of plastic surgery.

For vanity purposes? Or to change his look and elude authorities?

She wasn't sure.

Either way, bile churned inside her at the sight of the man . . . the man who'd tried to kill her mother. She wanted to lunge across the desk. To give him a piece of her mind.

Instead, she tried to look grateful. To make it seem as if he'd saved her. Like she was on his side.

She swallowed hard as her cover story flashed back to her. She couldn't blow this.

"Thank you so much for saving me." Her voice cracked with emotion. "I didn't know who else to turn to, and I panicked."

Rafferty nodded slowly, his face not showing any emotion. Instead, he leaned back in his seat. A closed laptop sat in front of him, as well as an old-fashioned desk phone.

Why would he have an old phone like that? She couldn't be sure.

Other than those two things, there was nothing personalizing the space—no pictures or decorations. No awards.

Just blank, white walls.

"Why don't you have a seat?" Rafferty nodded at the chair on the other side of his desk. "Grab a bottle of water from the mini fridge in the corner. Then tell me exactly what happened so we can figure out who did this. We have no time to waste."

She grabbed a bottle and took a long sip. Then she sat across from Rafferty and wiped a droplet of water from her mouth with the sleeve of her sweatshirt.

His intense gaze bore holes into her as he remained all-business. "We need to get down to business. Who grabbed you?"

"I have no idea who it was. . ." Heidi shook her head, still breathing heavily. She'd drunk so much water so quickly that she had to catch her breath.

Almost as if he hadn't heard her, he said, "Some men are out to get you as revenge on me. I need you to tell me exactly what happened so I can figure out which of my enemies it was."

Heidi swallowed hard at his words. "Earlier, you said you thought it was Stephen."

"Was it?"

She shook her head. "No, I didn't recognize these men."

"Tell me about them."

She ran through the cover story. How she and Donald had been run off the road. How strange men had grabbed her. Put her in their Camry. Taken her to a house in the middle of nowhere.

Then she'd said how they'd left her alone for a few minutes. How she'd seen the opportunity to run, so she had.

But she'd gotten lost in the woods. She'd had to spend the night. Had started again in the morning.

Until she stumbled upon the small town of Norton and had called Rafferty.

"Sounds terrifying," Rafferty murmured, not quite sounding compassionate.

"Who exactly are these enemies of yours? Why are they coming after me?"

"I know you want answers, but I'm afraid I can't tell you that."

"Why not? Why can't I know what's going on?"

"The important thing is that you're safe now. We'll give you clean clothes, food, and a place to sleep."

"For how long?" she asked.

"For as long as necessary." He glanced at the time on his watch and stood. "We need to talk more.

However, I have a phone call I need to take. We'll debrief more later. In the meantime, Edward will show you to your accommodations."

"But—"

Before she could say anything else, Edward escorted her away.

This wasn't the way Heidi had envisioned their talk going.

She was going to have to be proactive if she wanted to find out answers.

———

Stephen continued to spout directions as Gage drove.

They were close to the spot where Heidi's tracker had last pinged. But the longer the radio silence lasted, the tighter the muscles across his chest grew.

The fact Stephen couldn't hear anything anymore wasn't a good sign.

He wanted—no, make that *needed*—to know Heidi was okay.

As the dirt road continued to narrow, Gage pulled into the woods. They would have to go the rest of the way on foot to avoid being seen.

Wasting no time, they headed toward the location where Heidi had recently been.

Finally, the trees cleared.

He and Gage paused.

A shack stood in front of them—one that didn't look big enough to hold but only a few people at the most. It wasn't the type of place Rafferty would want to stay. In the distance stood a dilapidated barn. They saw no cars or other vehicles.

Something wasn't adding up, and he didn't like it.

Stephen had known this plan was a bad idea. Being here right now only proved it.

A sense of panic—something he rarely felt—filled him, tried to make his bones quiver. So much about this situation was out of his control, and he hated the helpless feeling plaguing him.

"There's an explanation for this." Gage rubbed his neck as he stared at the shack. "We just need to think it through more."

"Yes, we do." He started to step forward when Gage grabbed his arm and stopped him.

"Probably not a good idea."

He stiffened. "What do you mean?"

"We're both logical enough to know that Heidi and those men didn't disappear into thin air. Something isn't as it seems. If Rafferty is the man I think he is, there could be cameras or booby traps set up. We don't want to show our hand yet."

"But Heidi—"

Gage's gaze burned into his. "Let's just take a deep breath before we make any decisions."

Stephen started to rebuke Gage's statement but then clamped his mouth shut instead.

Gage was right. Stephen couldn't let his emotions get in the way.

But he could hear a time bomb ticking in his head —and that was powerful enough to make his nerves explode.

CHAPTER
THIRTY-THREE

EDWARD HAD ESCORTED Heidi from Rafferty's office, which was unfortunate since she already didn't like the man.

She'd been taken to a windowless bedroom. This place was most likely designed to survive a nuclear fallout, so she shouldn't be surprised.

There was no attached bathroom, just a metal bed with a white bedspread and a dresser. She'd checked under the bed and in the dresser.

Nothing in the room alarmed her.

At least, the space was clean.

However, the whole situation gave her chills.

In fact, this bunker felt more like a grave.

The good news was that Rafferty had seemed to buy her story. She hadn't seen any hints of suspicion in his gaze. But she'd still need to proceed with caution.

The man was sly, a trained interrogator and mastermind of a super soldier program.

She couldn't afford to let down her guard.

Yet she also knew she didn't have much time.

She sat on the edge of the bed and hit the button on her shoe as Cynthia had shown her.

The secret compartment opened. She pulled the cell phone out and touched the screen.

Her heart beat harder. There wasn't a signal down here.

Did that mean Stephen and Gage couldn't track her? That they couldn't hear what was being said?

She'd known that was a possibility. But still . . .

Her throat tightened as panic tried to take over.

She hoped Stephen and Gage had been able to hear what was said earlier, at least. But now she was underground. Rock surrounded this mountain. Metal surrounded the bunker.

What were the chances a signal could get through?

Not good.

Yet Rafferty seemed to have some type of internet connection. He had a computer set up and had mentioned taking a phone call. So clearly there was some way to communicate despite their surroundings.

She sat on her bed and took a deep breath. Rafferty had instructed her to relax. But there was no way she could rest. She had too much on her mind. Too many questions.

Where did she even start?

Was this Rafferty's headquarters? He did have an office here.

This all seemed strategic. This was the perfect location for him to plan all his deeds without being caught.

She froze when she heard a metal door scrape open somewhere in the hallway. Heard footsteps.

Someone spoke. She recognized that voice.

Rafferty. He'd left his office and was headed somewhere else.

Maybe this was her opportunity to explore, to find out more information.

She waited until the footsteps passed.

Then she cracked her door open and peered out.

The hallway was empty.

Rafferty hadn't told her to stay in her room. Hadn't locked her inside. Would it look suspicious if she decided to explore? She could always say she was looking for a bathroom if she were caught.

She had to be smart about this.

She lifted a quick prayer.

Then she slipped from the room and started down the hall.

With every step, she asked God to help her find whatever information she needed.

———

Heidi stared at Rafferty's office, a room she'd already been in. Yet the space felt foreign.

Thankfully, she'd seen Edward punch in the code earlier. For that reason, she'd been able to get inside.

She didn't know how much time she had. So where did she even start?

Rafferty's desk made the most sense. Really, there was nowhere else. No filing cabinet or anything else where information might be stored. That seemed strange. He would need records of things—unless they were all electronic.

She couldn't be sure.

Of course, she did have some files at her office. Maybe Rafferty didn't feel the need to keep his own records.

Yet that didn't seem like Rafferty. He was a control freak.

Working quickly, she went to the other side of the desk and began opening drawers.

But there was nothing in his desk except what she'd expected—a few office supplies like Post-it notes and pens. His checkbook, which boasted the address of their office in Atlanta. Some breath mints.

There were no files stashed in the drawers. Rafferty was too smart to leave a paper trail.

But wasn't he too smart to leave a digital trail as well?

Whatever information he had, he would keep it secure.

Exactly how would he do that? *The element of surprise is your friend. The unexpected can work to your advantage.*

Rafferty had often said those words. Now, Heidi needed to think like he did.

She straightened and glanced around. Was there some kind of hidden space in here? There were no pictures to look behind. No plants to look under.

She ran her hand along the cement block wall. If she pressed on the right brick, would a secret compartment be revealed?

The idea seemed crazy.

She tried anyway, halfway expecting a brick to pop out and reveal some hidden files.

They didn't.

The floor was concrete. There were no rugs to search under either.

The only other thing was the mini fridge.

She opened the door. Only water was inside.

She looked behind it. Again, nothing.

She nibbled on her bottom lip as she fought frustration.

She'd risked everything to come here and find information. She had to do everything in her power to succeed.

Just then, a noise sounded in the hallway.

Footsteps, she realized.

Panic raced through her.

There was only one place in the room she could hide.

Underneath the desk.

But if Rafferty came in and sat down, she'd be a goner.

Still, right now, she had no choice but to try, especially as the footsteps came to a stop outside the door.

CHAPTER
THIRTY-FOUR

HEIDI PULLED her knees to her chest and hardly allowed herself to breathe.

Someone was standing outside the office.

The knob rattled. A second later, the door opened.

Her worst fears were confirmed: Someone was inside the office with her. Someone with heavy steps. A man.

The next few minutes would determine her future.

She pressed her eyes shut, wishing she could disappear. But that wasn't a possibility.

The man paced closer.

Who was here? What was he doing? For some reason, she didn't think it was Rafferty. It seemed as if Rafferty would walk in with a purpose. Come straight to the desk.

This person seemed to be checking something out. Had someone noticed she was gone from her room? Was this person looking for her?

She hadn't moved anything in the office. If this man was searching for anything out of place, nothing should alarm him. Heidi only hoped he didn't walk to the other side of the desk.

As the footsteps moved, she pulled her eyes open again.

Something above her caught her eye.

She blinked in surprise.

Something was taped to the bottom of the desk.

A legal-size envelope had been secured with masking tape there.

Her heart skipped a beat. Why would an envelope be taped there?

She knew: to conceal its contents.

She had to see what was inside.

Later.

The footsteps came closer. Closer.

Then the man paused behind the desk.

The office chair concealed her. But all he had to do was to pull it out and . . .

She swallowed hard. She didn't want to think about it.

Instead, she studied the man's legs.

This wasn't one of Rafferty's men. They always wore the same utility-style cargo pants and boots.

This person wore black dress slacks and pristine leather shoes.

She couldn't see his face. Not without leaning out and peering up—and she couldn't chance that.

Whoever it was, he lingered by the desk.

What was he doing?

Why didn't he just leave?

Then he slowly began to pull the chair out.

———————

Stephen stood behind a cluster of trees looking at the shack in front of them. His muscles tightened so much that they ached.

How much longer could he stand here and wait? He and Gage had examined the area for cameras. They'd found several and had made sure to avoid them.

They'd checked out the barn. Inside, two SUVs had been stashed in the shadows.

They'd put a tracker on both vehicles, so if anyone left, they could follow.

But that didn't tell him what was going on inside the shack. The cameras were aimed at the door to the place, so they couldn't afford to get close.

He hated not knowing what was going on. The proactive side of him wanted to act, to do something. But experience told him to wait.

He glanced at Gage, grateful that his colleague was more level-headed right now. "What's our plan?"

"We're going to need to play this by ear." Gage's gaze remained fixed on the distance. "If we walk out there and Rafferty is watching, this whole operation will be over."

Stephen glanced at his laptop again, wishing he could hear whatever Heidi was hearing. But their signal was still gone. The microphone they'd planted on Heidi had done no good.

Gage seemed to read his thoughts as he said, "We just need to give it a little more time. Then maybe someone will show their hand."

As if right on cue, the door to the shack opened. A man Stephen didn't recognize stepped out, dressed in cargo pants and a black T-shirt.

"Who is that?" he muttered.

"Never seen him before," Gage said. "Let's see what he's doing."

The man paced a few steps away from the shack.

Then he paused and scanned the area.

Stephen slipped behind a tree.

Had this guy received intel indicating Stephen and Gage were out here? Was he looking for them now?

If so, he and Gage would have to figure out another plan before they all got killed.

CHAPTER
THIRTY-FIVE

HEIDI STARED at the desk chair as it rolled away from her.

Then it stopped. All someone had to do was sit down, and she'd be spotted.

She held her breath.

At any minute, she fully expected the man to find her. To draw his gun and . . .

She swallowed hard, trying to push the image out of her mind.

But the man didn't try to sit.

What was he doing?

Then movement sounded.

"Don't worry," a deep voice said. "I'm handling it."

The voice sounded familiar. Where had she heard it before?

And exactly what was this guy handling?

"I've got things under control. The plan will go off without a hitch. You have my word."

Finally, he took a step away.

But Heidi didn't dare relax.

She waited instead. Listened as the footsteps grew farther and farther away.

The door opened. The man stepped out. A click sounded as the door closed and locked.

He was gone.

She released a pent-up breath.

Remaining beneath the desk, she carefully pulled the envelope down and opened it.

A single piece of paper was inside.

Knoxville 10/10
    Nashville 10/12
    Johnson City 10/14
    Memphis 10/15
    Chattanooga 10/15
    Clarksville 10/16

She frowned. What was the significance of this? It had to be important.

Instead of keeping the paper, Heidi pulled the

phone from her shoe and took pictures of it. She couldn't trust her memory with these details, and they might be too important to forget.

Working quickly, she put the envelope back as she'd found it and then scooted the chair out. She cautiously rose, halfway expecting a gotcha moment.

None came.

Still, she didn't know how much time she had. She had to get out of here.

She started to step away when she spotted the phone on Rafferty's desk.

Her breath caught, and she paused.

It was an old-fashioned landline.

Her heart pounded in her ears as she considered her options.

Leave now before she was caught? Or take a risk and call Stephen?

She didn't have to think long. She had to call Stephen. After all, he had no idea what was happening right now. If Stephen and Gage barged in on her in this bunker, she might lose her opportunity to find out any more information.

That settled it.

Working quickly, she found his number on her phone and dialed.

As she gripped the phone, she prayed he'd answer . . . before anyone caught her in this room.

———

Stephen remained behind the tree, still frozen.

The slightest movement could give away his presence, and he couldn't chance that.

Gage did the same behind another tree nearby.

What was that man doing?

When they heard nothing for several moments, Stephen finally dared to peer around the tree.

The man still stood there. But now he smoked a cigarette.

Stephen almost wanted to laugh.

The guy was taking a smoke break.

Their presence here hadn't been discovered.

He watched the man another moment. The guy finished his cigarette, then dropped it on the ground and stomped it out.

As he glanced around again, Stephen slipped back behind the tree.

When he looked again, the man had headed back to the shack.

Stephen released the breath he'd been holding.

He was still ready to charge into that building. It took every ounce of his self-control not to. But he forced himself to wait.

Something vibrated in his pocket. His phone, he realized.

He snatched it and looked at the screen. It was an unknown number.

But only a few people had his number, and Heidi was one of them.

Making the split-second decision, he answered.

"Stephen?" a soft voice whispered on the other end.

His grip on the phone tightened as his heart rate surged. "Heidi? Are you okay? What's going on?"

Gage moved closer, a knot between his eyes.

"I'm okay," she told him. "There's no cell service inside. There's a bunker beneath that shack, and it's set up complete with places to sleep and an office."

He'd figured that much. "Is Rafferty onto you?"

"I don't think so. I snuck into his office—"

"You did what?" His voice rose with apprehension.

"I did what I was supposed to do. I don't have much time to explain myself to you."

Stephen clamped his mouth shut and didn't say anything else, knowing her words were true. Still, if she made one wrong move . . .

He swallowed hard. He didn't want to think about it.

"I found a list of cities and dates," she continued. "I don't know what they mean, but they must be important. Rafferty had them hidden beneath his desk."

A surge of admiration rushed through him. "Good work. What are they?"

She rattled the names and numbers off to him.

"You've done what you went in to do," Stephen told her. "Now we need to get you out of there."

"I'm not sure that's going to be possible." Her voice trembled. "Not yet at least."

His heart beat harder. "It's not safe. If Rafferty catches wind of any of this—"

"I know. But I just need you to trust me. Give me a couple more hours."

That sounded like a terrible idea. "But—"

"I can't talk anymore," she rushed. "Just give me two hours. I'll make it work."

Then the line went dead.

Stephen stared at the phone, resisting the urge to throw it onto the ground in frustration.

That would do him no good. It would only cut off any more communication with Heidi. But at least they had something to work with now.

He relayed the conversation to Gage.

Then they called Larchmont to tell him the update.

CHAPTER
THIRTY-SIX

HEIDI PUT THE PHONE BACK, satisfied she'd done the right thing.

Now she had to get out of this office without being caught. That could prove to be difficult.

She crept toward the door, trying to stay light on her feet.

Her lungs were so tight she could hardly breathe as she paused. On the count of three, she cracked the door open. Peered out.

She halfway expected to be bum-rushed.

Instead, she saw no one.

If she was going to move, it needed to be now.

Quickly, she stepped out and closed the door behind her. She hurried down the hall, trying to move fast but appear casual.

She thought she was doing well . . . until Edward stepped out from one of the nearby rooms into the hallway.

Her pulse quickened as soon as she saw him.

He strode toward her, his eyes narrowed with suspicion. "What are you doing?"

"Looking for the bathroom."

He eyed her another moment.

Did he believe her?

Or did he know she'd been in the office? Heidi hadn't even thought to look for cameras.

What if this hallway was monitored?

Her throat tightened.

She stared up at Edward, trying not to show her panic. *Stay calm, Heidi. Calm. The testing of your faith develops perseverance. Persevere now!*

Edward continued to stare at her as if sizing her up. Finally, he nodded at a door in the distance. "The bathroom is over there. I thought I told you."

Her lungs loosened but only for a moment. The situation was still dire.

"You thought wrong." Heidi nodded at him before stepping toward the door.

"Rafferty wants to see you for dinner in five minutes," Edward called. "I'll wait out here for you."

Another tremble raked through her. "If that's what he wants."

She had to seem compliant. Grateful to be here and to have been rescued by Rafferty.

She slipped into the bathroom and locked the door behind her. Then she splashed some water on her face.

The liquid felt nice as it cooled her burning face. Then she found a clean towel under the sink and pressed the soft fabric against her face.

Only then did she look in the mirror.

She frowned.

She really did look like a wreck. Her hair sprang out from her ponytail in different directions. Dirt smudged her cheeks. Circles hung beneath her eyes.

Working quickly, she pulled her hair into a bun and tried to make herself more presentable. She brushed a leaf from her sweatshirt, swept some dirt from her shoulder, and drew in several deep breaths.

She couldn't buy any more time.

She glanced at herself once more in the mirror.

She could do this. She'd come this far. She couldn't fail now.

She stepped out and, just as Edward had promised, he waited for her.

He gave her another scathing look before escorting her down a hallway into another room.

When he opened the door, a dining/living room combination greeted her.

The area still looked cold and sterile with plain white walls. A sturdy wooden table added a little life to the space. But the black couches and concrete floor offset any homey feelings—as did the danger surrounding her.

Rafferty sat at the table, a salad in front of him.

There didn't appear to be a kitchen here. And how much electricity could be run to this place without tipping someone off that it was here? Or maybe it was on a generator.

It didn't matter either way.

Those things were the least of Heidi's concerns right now. She wasn't sure why her mind had gone there. It was her attention to details, she supposed. That had made her good at her job.

"Sit." Rafferty nodded to the seat in front of him.

Edward nudged her forward, and Heidi sat, just as directed.

Another man appeared and placed a premade salad in front of her. She thanked him and took the plastic lid off.

Spinach, grilled chicken, blueberries, and almond slivers.

Her stomach growled.

She really did need to eat. She'd been starving earlier, but the stress of the situation had gotten to her. Still, she needed food for energy.

"Thank you for the salad." She lifted a plastic fork.

Something about the setup left her feeling unsettled.

Who had Rafferty spoken with on the phone when he'd excused himself from their conversation earlier? Why did the man want to see her now? Was he onto her?

Her heart pounded harder.

She cleared her throat. "By the way, Monarch has been trying to get in touch with you. He said you weren't answering."

"I'm done with that man."

Heidi raised an eyebrow. "I thought you were allies."

"He's chosen his side."

She wasn't sure what that meant. Before she could ask, Rafferty changed the subject.

Rafferty leveled his gaze with her. "I know what you've been up to, Heidi. You and I need to talk."

A tremble raked through Heidi.

This was it, wasn't it? The moment when the truth came out.

The moment she might die.

————

Stephen kept an eye on the time.

It had almost been two hours. That was what Heidi had asked for.

In only five more minutes, that time would be up.

He and Gage had already discussed their plan of action.

They'd called Larchmont, and he was sending backup. They couldn't take down this operation alone.

But they could breach this bunker. Search the place for Heidi. Rescue her.

Best-case scenario, they could get her out without being seen. However, that was unlikely. They'd be in unfamiliar territory, which would be a huge disadvantage. They had no idea what they'd be up against inside that bunker.

Worst-case scenario, they'd be spotted. Gunfire would erupt. The most skilled operatives would win.

However, death never seemed like a win.

Stephen and Gage had been left with little choice right now.

They'd researched the dates and cities Heidi had told them about. So far, they hadn't been able to link the times and places with anything or anyone in particular. But Larchmont had some people working on it.

Gage glanced at his watch and then looked at Stephen. "You ready to move in?"

Stephen nodded. "I've been ready."

"Then let's go."

But just as they took a step toward the shack, the door opened.

Stephen and Gage slid back behind the trees and out of sight.

He watched as Heidi stepped out, three men flanking her.

Two guards.

And Rafferty.

Gage snapped some pictures on his phone to send to the team.

Stephen couldn't take his eyes off Heidi. She'd changed clothes and cleaned up. But her eyes darted around as if she was looking for them. She didn't look frantic, but there was definitely a touch of fear in her gaze.

A knot formed in Stephen's throat.

Should he step in? Or let this play out as planned?

"We'll follow them," Gage said quietly. "We need to see where they're going."

The knot grew larger.

He knew his colleague's choice was correct. But that didn't mean he liked it.

An SUV pulled from the barn, and Rafferty, Heidi, and one of the men climbed inside.

Where were they taking her?

Stephen glanced at Gage, an unspoken conversation passing between them.

They needed to get back to their vehicle so they could follow.

CHAPTER
THIRTY-SEVEN

ANXIETY THRUMMED INSIDE HEIDI.

Rafferty hadn't explained his statement about knowing what she'd been up to. Instead, he'd directed her to listen to his instructions. They needed to leave, and she needed to change clothes first—no questions asked.

To her surprise, he had some clothing already purchased in her size. Heidi wasn't sure how that was even possible. But Rafferty didn't seem willing to answer questions.

She'd asked if she could wear her tennis shoes, and he'd given her a flat no. She could see why. They were dirty and grungy.

Some dress slacks, a cream-colored blouse, and shiny loafers had been laid out for her. Something much more professional.

But she hated to leave her cell phone behind. Should she take the cell phone out of her sneakers? Maybe she could slide it into her pocket.

That was risky, however. If she was caught with the device . . . they would probably kill her right on the spot.

She'd known what her decision had to be.

She'd showered, fixed her hair, and dressed. She glanced in the mirror and gave herself a nod of approval. However, she could see the fear lingering in her gaze. She prayed Rafferty couldn't see it, that he didn't read too much into it.

A knock sounded at the door. "Time to go."

It was Edward.

She stepped toward the door. As she did, she glanced back at her shoes one more time.

Those were her lifeline, her connection with the outside world.

She'd be going solo from here out.

She prayed she knew what she was doing. However, at this point, she had no other choice.

She opened the door, and Edward scowled. "About time."

He took her arm—a little too tightly—and began pulling her down the hallway. "Is this really necessary?"

He only grunted in return, and his grip didn't loosen.

As they passed Rafferty's office, he stepped out and joined them.

Her heart continued to pound in her ears with every step. She had no idea what might happen next. Part of her didn't want to find out.

Dear Lord, help me. Please!

Edward escorted her out of the bunker, up the stairs, and into the shack.

An SUV waited for them outside.

"Get in," Edward muttered.

She glanced at the woods surrounding them. Was Stephen out there watching?

She didn't see him. But her gut told her he was there.

A touch of reassurance filled her at the thought.

Before she could ask questions, Edward shoved her inside. Rafferty climbed in up front beside another man she hadn't seen before, and Edward sat beside her. The third man stayed behind.

A bad feeling continued to rumble inside her as they pulled away.

"Where are we going?" Her voice trembled as her nerves got the best of her.

"It's not important," Rafferty said over his shoulder in the front seat.

He grabbed his phone and hit a button. She listened closely as someone answered.

"Is everything arranged?" Pause. "This needs to go off without a hitch." Another pause. "We'll be there in an hour."

He was definitely lining up something, but Heidi wasn't sure what.

Whatever was happening, she was certain it wasn't a good thing.

The only thing she could do at this point was play it by ear, and that seemed like a terrible plan.

———

As soon as Stephen and Gage had seen Heidi get into the SUV, they'd hurried through the woods to their own vehicle. Stephen opened his computer and pulled up the tracker, determined not to lose track of where Heidi was headed.

He frowned as he stared at the screen. "Her tracker is offline. It shows she's still at the bunker."

"That's not a surprise," Gage said. "They had her change clothes."

Stephen had known that was true. But he still hated the fact he was cut off from her. The good news was that they'd placed a tracker in the wheel well of the SUV she was in. They wouldn't be able to hear her conversation, though.

He couldn't imagine where they might be headed, but he was about to find out.

His phone buzzed, and he saw it was Larchmont.

"I have an update for you," Larchmont started. "The team has been trying to cross-reference those cities and dates you sent me. We finally have a lead. It appears this is the schedule for Commander George Billings, the times he'll be on the road campaigning in those cities."

George Billings? Stephen tried to recall everything he knew about the man.

The man had also worked for the Joint Chiefs of Staff, hadn't he? And he was running for senator in Tennessee. That was all Stephen could remember.

Why would Rafferty care about this commander?

He narrowed his eyes with thought. "Okay . . . so Rafferty and his men are tracking this guy's campaign?"

"It appears they are." Larchmont paused. "But I have reason to believe Commander Billings is the one who gave the final okay to Project Elevate."

Stephen's thoughts raced. "I thought that was Commander Davis?"

"So did I. But we were wrong," Larchmont said. "There was more going on than we realized. Cynthia had to deal with Billings on more than one occasion when she was a lobbyist, and she said the man is no good. He's power hungry and has said on several occasions that he'd like to be president of the United States one day."

"You think Commander Billings is being targeted because of his involvement in Project Elevate?" Stephen clarified.

"Rafferty is going to send his men after Commander Billings. If the commander tells people about Project Elevate, Rafferty will be painted in a worse light than he already is. He'll be on wanted lists, and the feds will make it their goal to find him and bring him down—especially when they learn he's still operating. He's playing a very dangerous game."

"But Billings's campaign would be ruined if he spoke the truth," Gage said.

"Yes, that's absolutely true. There's still more here we need to uncover."

"You can say that again," Stephen muttered as they continued down the narrow mountain road.

They couldn't lose sight of that SUV, yet they couldn't be seen either. The situation was precarious at best. Even though they'd placed a tracker on the SUV, they needed to be careful. Heidi's life depended on it.

"One other thing," Larchmont said. "We were able to identify the man in the photo Gage sent us—the guy who was smoking outside the shack."

"Who is he?" Stephen stiffened. "I didn't recognize him from Blackstone."

"He actually works for an organization called Dagger."

Stephen's jaw tightened at the mention. "I've heard of them. They're another security group—an unscrupulous one, at that."

"They're nothing but trouble. They're the men people hire when they need someone with no moral compass. I don't know how they're affiliated with all of this. But whatever the connection, it's not good."

So why was Rafferty taking Heidi with him to wherever he was going? That was one other thing that didn't make sense.

Unless Rafferty somehow wanted to use Heidi as a fall guy.

Was that it? Was Heidi going to be the scapegoat for whatever scheme Rafferty had devised? The person who looked guilty of plotting an assassination?

There were still some uncertainties with that theory. But nothing else made sense.

However, Stephen prayed he was wrong.

CHAPTER
THIRTY-EIGHT

AS SOON AS Rafferty got off the phone, Heidi dove into her questions again. "Where are we going?"

He narrowed his eyes. "You ask too many questions. It's not important."

"It must be kind of important if I had to dress up."

He let out a long breath. "Please, stop asking so many questions."

Subtle warning stained his voice.

Heidi started to ask more questions before thinking better of it and clamping her mouth shut.

She didn't want to push him too much. Besides, it wasn't as if once she found out information she'd be able to pass it on to Stephen. Her only hope was that Stephen was somehow tracking her now.

She'd glanced at the road behind her a couple of times and didn't see anyone. She didn't want to be too obvious, however.

Instead, she watched the miles as they blurred past. They were going farther and farther away from the shack. As they did, more signs of life appeared.

She had to work hard to keep the tremble inside her from emerging.

All things considered, Rafferty had to know she'd be a little nervous, but she didn't want him to pick up on too many of her changing emotions. She couldn't raise his suspicions.

She'd made it this far. She couldn't blow it now.

They kept driving. Rafferty had already spoken with various people on the phone. But he was always certain to mumble to the extent she couldn't understand what he said. But he'd said something about meeting someone. Having things in place. Making sure everything was ready.

Something was going down tonight, wasn't it? But what?

And why did Rafferty want her with him now?

A street sign in the distance caught her eye.

Knoxville. They were headed toward Knoxville.

Knoxville . . . that had been one of the cities on the list she'd seen.

And if she remembered correctly, the date listed beside Knoxville was . . . today.

Her heart thumped harder.

————

"Why are they going to Knoxville?" Stephen watched Rafferty's vehicle turn toward the city.

"Knoxville was on the list," Gage reminded him.

"You're right . . ." Stephen sucked in a breath. "Does that mean that Commander Billings will be there?"

"It makes the most sense."

"I've got to let Larchmont know." Stephen grabbed his phone.

He called Larchmont and told him his theory about where Rafferty was going with Heidi. Larchmont said he'd divert his guys toward that location instead of the shack.

"He's planning something with the commander," Larchmont muttered.

Stephen stared out the window at the buildings as they began popping up more frequently. "Are you thinking an assassination?"

"I think it's a possibility."

His mind continued to race. "But what reasons would Rafferty have to want to kill the commander?"

"Like I told you, the commander was associated with Project Elevate. I'm sure it goes back to that."

So this all tied in with Project Elevate and the commander who gave the go-ahead on the program's secret funding. Dagger had also gotten involved somehow.

Stephen tried to put the pieces together. Maybe Larchmont's theory was correct, and this was some type of assassination attempt.

However, Rafferty had people who did this for him. He didn't need to be there himself.

There was clearly more to this than met the eye.

They needed to be one step ahead of this guy if they had any hope of saving Heidi.

Stephen prayed they didn't arrive too late.

HEIDI'S EYES widened when she saw the vehicle turn toward the airport.

Instead of heading toward the entrance, they pulled behind the terminal to the area used by private planes.

The SUV came to a stop, and Edward jumped out and opened her door.

"You're coming with me," Rafferty muttered.

Edward grabbed her arm and pulled her out, leaving her no choice.

"Where are we going?" The question slipped out. "What are you planning exactly? You're scaring me."

Heidi glanced at the runway in the distance and saw that a plane had landed. Myriads of people had gathered on the other side of the fence to wait for it, almost as if someone important were in town. Men dressed in military uniforms waited inside the fence.

Instead of walking toward the crowd, Edward dragged her toward a smaller plane in the distance.

She stopped at the steps of the plane and turned to Rafferty. "We're flying somewhere?"

"Out of the country."

Her eyebrows shot up. "What? Why?"

"I'm going to be a wanted man very soon. People are after me and my team." His gaze met hers. "And they're after you, Heidi. Because of me."

"What do you mean, because of you? I know you said you've made a lot of enemies." Her voice sounded high-pitched as the words left her lips. "But why is someone after me? Why are you taking me with you?"

Rafferty's gaze locked with hers for a long moment. Finally, he cleared his throat and announced, "Because you're my daughter."

As the words echoed in her head, Heidi's world began to spin.

———

"Why are they going to the airport?" Stephen didn't bother to hide the confusion in his voice.

Gage pointed to a large private jet. "It looks like we have a special guest."

Stephen looked more closely. That was when he realized Commander Billings must have come into town on the aircraft.

All along he'd assumed Rafferty was headed to a campaign rally. But it appeared Rafferty was meeting the commander at the airport instead.

What exactly did Rafferty have up his sleeve?

His gaze went back to Rafferty's SUV.

Rafferty and Heidi climbed out. A man Stephen had seen multiple times gripped Heidi's arm, leading her to a smaller plane.

Wait . . . so Rafferty wasn't headed toward the commander? Then why was he here?

Stephen continued to scan the space. Movement on the outskirts of the airport caught his eye.

A glint of light on the rooftop of a nearby building.

Snipers, he realized.

What he didn't know was if these men were guarding the commander or if they were in position to take the commander out.

As Gage threw the SUV into Park, Stephen swerved his gaze between the commander and Heidi. Did the commander have any idea what was about to happen? His assassination could send serious shockwaves through the country. Could even cause conflict and violence to break out.

But Heidi's death . . . it would tear his personal world apart.

He could only get to one of them in time to save them.

Though more than anything he wanted to run to Heidi, the commander appeared to be in more imminent danger.

Either way, Stephen had to make a decision, and he had to make it quickly.

CHAPTER
FORTY

HEIDI'S MOUTH fell open as she stared at Rafferty on the steps. "What do you mean you're my father?"

"I loved your mother—so much that we had a child together. You."

She shook her head—and shook it hard. Rafferty couldn't be telling the truth. Maybe she heard him wrong. Maybe he was tricking her, lying.

"My dad died of a heart attack before I was born." Her voice sounded eerily calm. "He was an engineer. A good man."

"He was a weak man," Rafferty said. "Your mom wanted out of her marriage and was planning her escape. Then he died."

"Did you have anything to do with that?" Accusation stained her words. She wouldn't put it past Rafferty, especially not knowing what she did now.

"I did not." His words held no emotion. "Your mom and I were already together before that. We didn't want you to know I was your father. I thought you'd be in too much danger. I was right. Look at this situation now. It's dire."

"You're lying," Heidi barked, his statement finally hitting her and causing a surge of defensiveness to rise.

"I'm not. You have your mother's looks, but you have my intelligence and my eyes. You can't deny they're the same."

She stared into his green eyes, realizing the color was the same. But . . . "How do I know you're not wearing contacts?"

"I'm not. I did before to make you think they were brown."

Her lungs tightened until she could hardly breathe. What if he was telling the truth? What if her father was a monster? What did that make her?

She swallowed hard before asking, "Did you kill my mom?"

Nausea swirled inside her as she waited for the answer.

His expression remained unchanged. "It's complicated."

Revulsion swept through her, and she took a step back. "So, you did? I thought you said you loved her. How could you do something so horrible?"

"She walked in on a top-secret meeting and started asking too many questions. She should have just kept her head down. That was all I asked. She became a liability."

"And that's what you do to people who are liabilities? You kill them?" Emotion churned in her voice. How could she have been so clueless?

"I couldn't let her bring us down. I've worked too hard to get where I am. Too much is on the line."

Heidi's mind continued to race. "Just like the commander is trying to bring you down now? Is that why you're going to kill him?"

Rafferty narrowed his eyes and sighed. "We'll talk more on the plane. We don't have much time."

She shook her head, appalled at the very idea. "I can't go with you. You killed my mother. You hired me and didn't even tell me I was your daughter!"

"Please, Heidi." He sounded like an exasperated father, tired of his troublesome child.

The thought made her even more sick to her stomach.

At the sound of squealing tires, Heidi's gaze swerved to the side.

A black SUV pulled to a fast stop near the plane.

Was that Stephen? As if on cue, he stepped out.

"What's *he* doing here?" Rafferty muttered through clenched teeth.

"No idea," Edward muttered.

The good news was that meant Rafferty probably didn't know she and Stephen had been talking. Working together, essentially.

The element of surprise should work in their favor.

"We need to go," Rafferty muttered. "There's no time to waste."

Edward stepped closer, trying to nudge her onto the plane. But Heidi's feet remained planted.

Rafferty climbed up two steps and glanced back. "You can't stay here. We have to go. Now!"

She glanced back at Stephen as he stood near the SUV.

Stephen stared at her then looked at the commander. Then he glanced at the roof of the airport terminal.

Heidi followed his gaze and squinted as something in the distance glinted. Was that . . . a sniper?

Her breath caught.

She knew exactly the position Stephen was in.

Who did he save first?

"Heidi!" Rafferty called impatiently.

Heidi rubbed her chest, feeling that familiar

tension there as she fought against Edward, who tried to push her up the steps.

Rafferty stared down at her, realization rolling through his gaze.

"You would choose staying here rather than going with your own father?" Rafferty practically spit out the words, an edge of bitterness in his voice. "You have questions only I can answer. I've always looked out for you, Heidi. I've protected you, even if you didn't know it. I can protect you now too."

"Can you?" she asked. "Why are you here? Why are you running? Why should I believe a word you say?"

She needed to stop him. Needed to keep him here so the police could arrest him.

If she went with Rafferty on this plane, she'd never be seen again.

With that thought, she stepped back, her decision made.

But Edward blocked her escape, planting himself like a wall between her and Stephen.

———

Stephen stared at Heidi, his heart in his throat.

"Go to her," Gage said. "I'll handle things with the commander. Backup should be here any minute."

"You sure?" Stephen asked.

"Positive. Go!"

Gage didn't have to tell him again. Stephen took off toward Rafferty's plane.

Rafferty spotted him and had the man with him force Heidi up the steps. She dug in her heels. But the man was stronger than she was.

The guy tossed her over his shoulder. She kicked and squirmed, beating at the man's back. But it was no use.

The man lugged her up the steps and into the plane.

"No!" Stephen shouted.

He quickened his pace, desperate to get to her before the door closed and the plane took off.

Was Rafferty planning on leaving before anything happened with the commander? Stephen had assumed the man would want to stick around and see the assassination and the chaos afterward. He figured that would somehow bring him pleasure or satisfaction.

But seeing Stephen and Gage must have accelerated his flight plan.

Stephen couldn't let the door to the plane close. Rafferty's henchman still stood on the portable stairs. He reached for his waistband as he glanced at Stephen.

Then he drew a gun and raised it.

Stephen reacted quickly. He grabbed his gun, aimed, and fired.

The man moaned. Grabbed his shoulder. Then he fell from the stairway platform and hit the asphalt with a thud.

Stephen ran toward him. Kicked the man's gun away.

Then he ran back for the stairs.

As he did, a familiar figure peered out.

Rocky Velasquez.

The man must have been waiting on the plane.

Stephen couldn't let him stand in the way of rescuing Heidi.

CHAPTER
FORTY-ONE

HEIDI GLANCED at the man on the plane.

The man wearing a suit.

Rocky Velasquez, one of Rafferty's top agents. A man who'd also used the name Alfie in order to trick the men working for the Shadow Agency.

He was someone who'd do anything for Rafferty. Anything.

Stephen had taken Edward out. That was a relief.

But now there was Rocky.

"Take care of this!" Rafferty muttered as he sat in a seat and strapped his seatbelt over his waist. The only other person on the plane was the pilot.

Rafferty wanted to make a getaway involving only a few people. Probably smart.

But Heidi hoped that worked to his disadvantage right now.

Rocky stood at the door with his gun in hand.

At once, the reality of the situation hit her.

Stephen was determined to get to her, but in the process he could be killed.

She couldn't let that happen.

As Rocky tried to close the door, she threw all her weight into the man.

The gun flew from his hand and onto the tarmac. He stumbled back a couple of steps, clearly not expecting her move.

The interruption gave her just enough time to throw the door open.

As she did, she looked down at the ground. Saw they were moving. Saw how far it was for her to fall.

Her head began to spin.

"I was going to watch this play out," Rafferty muttered. "But there's no more time. Let's go!"

Was he talking to the pilot? Did Rafferty want to take off with the door open?

Heidi couldn't let that happen.

Stephen reached for her as the plane began to roll away from the stairway. "Heidi!"

Just as she stretched her arm toward him, Rocky came at her again. He grabbed her shoulder and pulled her back inside the plane with a grunt.

She landed on her butt, her palms softening the fall. But all she could think about was Stephen.

"What do you think you're doing?" Rocky's nostrils flared as he stared at her. "You stupid woman."

The next instant, Stephen propelled himself inside the plane. He landed on his side and quickly hopped to his feet. She wasn't sure where his gun was. Had he dropped it also? Was it in his waistband?

Rocky stared at him, his hands raised.

The two men began to circle each other.

In the distance, gunfire sounded.

Her heart rate ratcheted. Had the commander just been shot?

Sirens wailed.

Stephen and Rocky continued to face off as Rafferty sat in his seat.

The plane moved faster.

Heidi crawled out of the way.

As she did, she glanced at the open door.

The plane picked up speed.

If Stephen and Rocky didn't play it right, one of them could fall out that door.

She prayed that person wouldn't be Stephen.

———

Stephen faced off with Rocky, anger surging through his veins.

"You've been helping Rafferty this whole time, haven't you?" Stephen growled.

"It's an abomination what the military did to us," Rocky said, his fists also raised and ready to fight. "They need to pay. They treated us like we were disposable. Rafferty is the only one who's ever really cared."

"He only cares about himself." He moved to the side as he anticipated Rocky's next move.

"That's not true. We're like sons to him."

"If he had a choice of who to save, he'd always choose himself."

Rocky snarled. "You don't know that."

"I do. And so do you. You just don't want to admit it. You're disposable to Rafferty also, not just to the government."

"That's not true!" Rocky's pupils widened as fire seemed to ignite inside him.

"It is!"

The words spurred Rocky to action, and he took the first punch.

Stephen ducked, missing Rocky's hit.

Stephen swung back, and his fist connected with Rocky's jaw.

The man faltered, wincing with pain.

Then he sprang back to life and launched toward Stephen. The man caught him in a headlock.

Stephen used all his strength to propel Rocky over his shoulder.

The man landed with a thud on the floor.

Before he could get to his feet, Stephen grabbed his arms and flipped him over. He used some zip ties from his pocket to tie his hands together. Then he tied Rocky to a thick metal handle on the other wall.

"It didn't have to be with this way," Rocky muttered with a sneer. Blood drizzled from his nose and lip, but his eyes still looked feral. "You should have stayed on the right side."

"I *am* on the right side."

When Stephen looked up, Rafferty stood in the aisle glaring at him. He'd finally stood from his throne to join the fight.

"Why couldn't you just leave things alone? Let me go?" Rafferty raised his gun.

"No!" Heidi threw herself across the aisle until she stood in front of Stephen, her arms outstretched.

"Heidi . . . what are you doing?" Stephen started to move her aside. She was going to get herself killed.

She didn't budge and held her ground. "Rafferty won't shoot me."

He hated to break her confidence, but that assurance in her voice might get her killed. "I wouldn't be so sure of that."

"He won't. I'm . . . I'm his daughter."

Stephen's eyebrows shot up. Had he just heard her correctly?

He knew he had.

He would guess that update was news to Heidi also. He prayed she would have a chance to explain that more later. But survival was the most important thing right now.

Stephen stared at Rafferty. "I can't let your men kill the commander, no matter how much you think he deserves it. And I can't let you get away with this."

His eyes sparkled. "It's too late."

Heidi gasped. "What? He's already dead?"

"If everything went according to plan, then yes." Satisfaction stretched through Rafferty's gaze.

"You're not going to start a new life and take no culpability for this," Stephen growled. "I'll make sure of that."

"You know nothing," Rafferty barked. "All you are is a traitor. You're no better than him."

"You mean, the commander?" Stephen asked.

Rafferty sneered. "Yes, of course I'm talking about the commander. The mastermind of this whole program. The one who gave us authorization to proceed with it before turning on me."

"He fired you . . . so now you're trying to kill him?"

"It's a little more complicated than that."

"What are you talking about?" Stephen was in no mood to play guessing games right now.

"The truth is, it's kill or be killed." Rafferty's gaze hardened. "Billings has had his men trying to take *me* out. And I can't let him win."

CHAPTER
FORTY-TWO

HEIDI PAUSED, giving herself a second to let Rafferty's words sink in.

"You're saying the commander ordered Beau and Donald to be killed?" she asked. "You weren't behind that?"

"I was not," Rafferty said. "And, yes, Billings is the one trying to kill you as well. He had access to everything I did—though I tried to destroy it so he wouldn't have that power. He was able to track your every move through the GPS implanted in your shoulder."

"I thought that was your idea . . ." Heidi murmured.

"No, it was all Billings. He hired the men who flunked out of the program. He recruited them to join

Dagger, and then he hired Dagger to kill you. I was trying to save you!"

"Why would Billings go through all this trouble?" Stephen asked.

"Because if word gets out about what the commander authorized through Project Elevate, any hopes he has of winning this senate campaign would die. No one would vote for him."

"So he's trying to kill off everybody who was a part of the program?" Stephen asked.

Rafferty nodded. "Including me."

"So you're trying to kill him first?" Heidi was still trying to put all the pieces together. This wasn't her world. This wasn't the way she operated. The whole situation seemed so horrifying.

"If I don't, then he'd kill us," Rafferty said. "I'm just trying to watch out for my men."

The logic seemed twisted. Part of her admired Rafferty's loyalty to his men. But the other part of her wasn't so sure he was innocent in this.

"So you hired people to assassinate Commander Billings." Disgust lined Stephen's voice. "Then you came here to watch it happen and then fly away."

"As far as everyone at this airport knows, I'm not on this plane."

"Are those snipers yours or the commander's?"

Based on Rafferty's smirk, they were his.

Heidi glanced out the window as the plane taxied down the airstrip, picking up speed.

Her stomach lurched.

No . . .

The last thing she wanted was for them to take off.

Nothing good would come of it. If anything, she would just look complicit in this crime. Stephen also.

————

Rafferty wasn't going to use Heidi as a scapegoat. Stephen would make sure of that.

She was Rafferty's *daughter*?

Stephen's stomach churned with disgust at the thought—not disgust toward Heidi. Disgust toward Rafferty and all the damage he'd caused so many people.

When Larchmont had said that Heidi's mom worked for Rafferty, Stephen had no idea that had led to Heidi being born.

It brought the situation to an entirely different level.

How were they going to get out of this? Stephen couldn't exactly shoot Heidi's father. But he couldn't let this plane take off either.

"You've got to stop this plane," he told Rafferty.

'That's not going to happen." Rafferty glared at him.

"You're not going to get away with this."

"You might be surprised at what I'm able to get away with."

"Rafferty . . . Dad . . ." Heidi's voice cracked as she said that word. "Please, don't do this."

"There's a target on your head, too, Heidi. If I don't neutralize him, you won't ever be safe. Billings has too much riding on this."

"Don't pretend this is about her. You want to save your own skin." Stephen wanted to end this. Now. Before the man could do any more damage. "Don't you love her? She's your daughter."

"Of course, I love her!" Rafferty's eyes narrowed into tiny slits. "But it's too late. Everything is in place. The commander is dead. If he doesn't already have a bullet in his chest, he will soon. And there's nothing you can do to stop it."

CHAPTER
FORTY-THREE

HEIDI KNEW they didn't have much time.

The plane moved faster and faster.

The engines grew louder.

At any moment, they'd be airborne.

Just as the thought crossed her mind, the plane lifted.

They were taking off, she realized. It was too late to stop this!

She jostled backward, grabbing the seat beside her to keep her balance.

As she did, Rafferty stumbled toward her.

Stephen didn't miss a beat. He grabbed the man's gun. In two seconds flat, he had Rafferty subdued.

Rafferty might be brilliant, but he'd always relied on guards to keep him safe.

He had no one now.

Stephen handed his gun to Heidi and used a zip tie on Rafferty's hands.

She stared at the weapon, her eyes wide. What did he want her to do with this?

"You've got to get that pilot to land." Stephen locked gazes with her as he tightened the zip tie on Rafferty's wrists.

She stared at the weapon and felt it trembling in her hands.

But Stephen was right. She had no time to waste.

She turned and took a step into the cockpit, weapon still brandished. "Turn back to the airport. You need to land!"

"I don't take orders from you," the pilot scoffed.

"You don't understand." Heidi's voice sounded strong and bold, surprising even her. "This isn't a choice."

She pointed the weapon at the pilot.

The pilot glanced at her and then at the weapon as if checking to see if she was serious. "You're not going to pull that trigger."

"Maybe you're right." She shrugged. "Maybe it's not me you should be scared of."

"You talking about that guy back there?" He nodded toward Stephen.

"The former cage fighter? Maybe. But mostly I'm talking about the government. When they find out you were complicit in helping a wanted fugitive responsible for uncountable deaths escape the country, then you're going to jail for life too."

The first touch of doubt entered the pilot's expression. "You don't know what you're talking about."

"I don't know how much Rafferty is paying you," Heidi continued. "But I hope your life is worth it. Because you're going to say goodbye to it. The government will find you, and you'll pay for your part in this."

"I'm not doing anything wrong. I just took a job."

"You can keep telling yourself that. I think we both know that isn't true." She stared at the pilot, praying she'd gotten through to him.

They had to get this plane back on the ground.

She prayed things didn't turn more violent in the process.

————

Stephen had pushed Rafferty into a seat where he'd monitor him until they landed. Rocky was still tied to the handle in the distance, shouting and swearing.

Right now, the situation was under control.

He glanced at Rafferty again and shook his head.

The man was despicable. Selfish. Evil. Stephen couldn't believe he'd actually worked for this guy.

Thankfully, he'd seen the light before it was too late. He only wished he could say the same for his other former colleagues.

The plane shifted again as it banked right.

Stephen released his breath. Heidi had done it. She'd convinced the pilot to turn around.

Rafferty's eyes narrowed. He knew this was all over also, that his grand scheme wasn't going to work. Maybe he'd finally get the justice he deserved.

As they headed back toward the airport, Stephen glanced out the window.

Police cars had pulled up on the tarmac. Some kind of commotion was taking place near the other airplane. He wasn't sure exactly what was happening.

He prayed no one else had been hurt, that they weren't too late. However, he'd heard the earlier gunfire. He didn't know if someone had fired at the commander or if someone had taken down one of the snipers.

He waited as the plane landed.

As soon as it stopped, police cars surrounded them.

Stephen knew he had a lot of explaining to do.

But maybe this was all finally over.

CHAPTER
FORTY-FOUR

HEIDI RAN a hand over her face as exhaustion pressed on her.

The FBI had taken her in for questioning at least three hours ago. She'd lost track of time since coming to the field office. Needless to say, everyone had endless questions for her.

She could only imagine Stephen had also been sequestered. She hadn't seen him since the police had arrived on the scene and separated them.

Since then, she'd been trapped in this small room with multiple agents coming in and out, basically asking the same questions. Her adrenaline had worn off, and fatigue kicked in.

Now, she just wanted to climb into bed and sleep for a few days.

The important thing was that Rafferty hadn't gotten away with this. He'd been stopped in time.

But she hoped that her victory wasn't premature. That Rafferty hadn't laid the groundwork for her and Stephen to somehow still be found guilty in all this. She didn't think that was the case, but doubts still lingered in her mind.

She lifted her eyes as the door opened and yet another agent stepped inside. She was going to have to repeat herself again, wasn't she? How many more times would she have to go through this?

The agent stared at her before finally announcing, "You're free to go."

Her heart lifted. Had she heard him correctly? "Really?"

He nodded. "We verified your story, and it matches with everybody else's. We may have more questions for you later, but for now you can go." He paused. "And thank you for everything you did."

She offered a quick smile at his acknowledgement. "What about Rafferty?"

"He's been taken into custody, and he's facing a long list of charges for everything he's done. I have no doubt you'll be called to testify when this goes to trial."

"I'd be happy to do whatever I can to help." It didn't matter that the man was her father. He'd done terrible things, and now he needed to face the consequences.

"We appreciate your cooperation."

"And the commander?" Heidi hoped she wasn't pressing her luck by asking too many questions.

"Thanks to you, he's still alive. There was an assassination attempt that was thwarted. However, we believe the commander also hired people to take out Rafferty and his men, including you. We're still doing a deep dive into exactly what happened."

"I'm sure they told you this all goes back to Project Elevate—a program that the military sanctioned?"

The agent offered a quick nod. "Believe me, we're looking into all of it. Alan Larchmont has been a big help to us."

Heidi released the breath she'd been holding. Thank goodness. Maybe the worst of this was over.

She stood, her limbs shaky. She couldn't wait to get out of here. However, she didn't know exactly how she would leave. Call an Uber? Where would she even go tonight?

She wasn't sure about any of those things. But when she stepped out of the interrogation room, her eyes went to someone standing in the hallway waiting for her.

Stephen.

She ran straight into his arms.

His hug enveloped her, and she melted against him.

"It was you, wasn't it?" she muttered into his chest, suddenly stiffening.

"What do you mean? I've done a lot of things— some I want credit for and others I don't."

Her thoughts raced back to the times she'd been helped without realizing who was doing so. But now, she realized Stephen's woodsy scent had lingered behind sometimes. She didn't even make the connection until now that she was in his arms.

How could she have missed this earlier?

"You were the one who kept helping me out whenever trouble came my way, weren't you?" she practically whispered. "The one I called my guardian angel?"

How could she not have seen this before? Her eyes simply hadn't been open to the truth. But now she knew.

Long before all this drama broke out, Stephen had always been there.

Even more, he was still here with her now.

"More than anything, I've always wanted to keep you safe," Stephen murmured.

"Why didn't you tell me?" Heidi stared into his eyes as she waited for him to answer.

Stephen held Heidi tight. If he had his way, he'd never let go.

Her question lingered in his mind. *Why didn't you tell me?*

It was a good question.

He cleared his throat. "I don't know, really. I guess I knew I wasn't in a good place. But from the moment I met you in the office, I've been fascinated. Your exit interviews were always the highlight of my week."

"And you never said anything?"

He shrugged. "The truth is, I haven't dated much in the past several years because . . . no one ever compared to you."

"You should have told me."

"I knew I wasn't in the right place to be with anyone, especially you. I needed to make things right with myself, with God."

"But . . ." Her voice faded.

Probably because she knew his words were true.

He wasn't just talking about his emotional state. There was so much more to it than that. He'd been broken.

But not any longer. He'd gotten his act together. He knew what was in his power and what wasn't.

Now that Rafferty was out of his life, he truly had a chance to start fresh. To be his own person.

He leaned toward Heidi and pressed his lips onto the top of her head. He was no longer afraid of being the wrong man. Of being someone who could never be enough.

Heidi made him feel like a new man.

The two of them held each other for several more minutes.

Then Heidi suddenly stiffened. "The feds aren't arresting you, are they?"

"No." He shook his head. "You?"

"No. I think I might have to testify."

"I feel confident the worst of this is behind us. Now we can start rebuilding."

"Things could have turned out so differently." Her voice trembled. "I was so scared when we were on that plane."

"I had you then, and I've got you now."

She pulled away from his chest and looked into his eyes. His gaze was bloodshot and watery but strong. "You've always had my back, haven't you?"

"I'll never stop." Emotions made his voice hoarse.

As a smile spread across Heidi's face, Stephen did what he'd been wanting to do for a long time. He cupped her face in his hands and stared deeply into her beautiful green eyes.

Then he lowered his face until his lips met hers in what he hoped would be the first of many kisses.

CHAPTER
FORTY-FIVE

TWO WEEKS LATER, Larchmont called everyone for a meeting at his house in Tennessee.

It turned out the place didn't belong to him but to Cynthia. It had been easier for him to come here to recover than to go back to his home in Wyoming.

The whole gang had gathered. Gage. Austin. Trevor. Kai. Several other operatives Stephen hadn't met until today.

Stephen and Heidi were also there.

He was anxious to hear what Larchmont had to say.

Stephen was surprised he'd even been invited since he wasn't part of the original crew at the Shadow Agency. But apparently after everything that had happened, Larchmont considered Stephen an honorary member.

The past couple of weeks had been a whirlwind.

Stephen wished he could say all his time had been spent simply being with Heidi and getting to know her on a more personal level.

Unfortunately, his time had been filled with more questioning and developments. Heidi had especially been busy since she'd been Rafferty's assistant.

As far as Stephen could tell, the scales of justice appeared to be moving forward. Rafferty was still behind bars. Several of his men who were involved in the assassination attempt were also in jail awaiting trial.

Monarch had also been arrested. He'd been playing both sides. As a result, he'd made multiple enemies.

Rafferty had caught onto him and cut off contact. Then Monarch had realized the commander wanted to permanently silence him. In a panic, he'd tried to hire Blackstone.

He'd also tried to flee the country but had been stopped.

Commander Davis and Senator Wagner were also being questioned about their role in all this. So far, it didn't appear they'd done anything wrong.

Stephen had wondered if any of the past missions he'd done for Rafferty would land him behind bars. He'd wondered about the outcomes. About hidden motives and secret agendas. Maybe everything hadn't been on the up-and-up. But he'd been cleared.

He glanced at Heidi on the couch beside him. She stole a glance at him before reaching over and lacing her fingers between his.

Such a small action, yet her touch made him feel like he could conquer the world.

"Thank you to everyone for coming here today." Larchmont stood in front of them as they lounged on the couches and chairs in the massive living room.

Cynthia sat in a white leather chair up at the front also, her legs crossed in a demure fashion as she looked up at her husband and listened to everything he said.

The man was already so much stronger, and his face wasn't as pale. He was recovering nicely.

"I know things have been crazy here recently, and I know you all have a lot of questions," Larchmont continued. "But I thought that rather than addressing you each individually, we should have a meeting where I can tell everyone at once."

Everyone waited for him to continue.

He drew in several breaths, a tortured look in his eyes. "I know I didn't tell you everything that was going on with Project Elevate. I suppose I thought I was protecting you by not disclosing everything, but I can clearly see now I was wrong. Rafferty and I had different visions for what Project Elevate should be, and Rafferty eventually went off the deep end. When he left, I tried to keep as many of the men with me as I could. But some chose to go with Rafferty."

He looked at Stephen, who nodded. His assessment was correct. Rafferty had claimed the military didn't care about them. That leaders were going to ship the guys from Project Elevate off on impossible missions they were sure not to survive.

He'd insisted that coming with him was the better, more sensible choice. The man had become a father figure to some of them—a poor representation of a father, but they'd had no one else.

Rafferty had been very convincing. He'd painted the program and Larchmont in a bad light.

"I tried to shape the program into what it was originally supposed to be," Larchmont paused, his voice becoming garbled with emotion. Cynthia nodded at him, urging him to go on. After gathering himself another moment, he did. "But then I began to see the error of our ways. I saw how taking people, no matter how broken, and trying to make them into a machine-like soldier was wrong. I urged the government to shut the program down. And they did. That was when I took you guys with me and started the Shadow Agency. I didn't want to leave you guys hanging out to dry."

"Are we sure it's been shut down?" Gage asked.

A shadow passed over Larchmont's eyes. "From everything I've been told, it has been. As of right now, I have no reason to believe Project Elevate is still in operation."

But Stephen knew that no one knew about the original program either. If the government was continuing this program, they wouldn't tell anyone about it.

The thought left him unsettled.

"If I could go back and do things differently, I would," Larchmont said. "I suppose hindsight is always twenty-twenty."

Stephen agreed with that assessment. If only he'd known what Rafferty had been up to, he wouldn't have stayed with him for as long as he did.

"The good news is that Rafferty and Commander Billings will be going away for a long time. The commander knew if Rafferty were to spill the beans about his involvement in Project Elevate then his senate campaign would be over. That's why he decided to try to eliminate Rafferty and anyone affiliated with him." Larchmont glanced at Heidi. "That's where you came in. That's why Beau and Donald were both killed. That's why Billings sent those men to kill you as well."

Heidi cast a grateful smile at Stephen. "If you hadn't been there, then I would be dead."

Stephen squeezed her hand harder, not liking that thought.

"Rafferty found out about what was going on and decided to get revenge," Larchmont said. "He arranged the assassination attempt on the commander, and he was going to flee the country."

"And leave the rest of his guys behind," Stephen added.

"Rafferty tends to only think about himself." Larchmont paused and drew in another breath as if shifting his thoughts. "And that leaves us where we are now. With everything that's happened, I understand if you all want to leave the Shadow Agency."

"Is there anything else we need to know?" Austin asked.

Larchmont shook his head. "I've told you everything I know. No more secrets."

Silence stretched a moment.

Then Gage said, "I'm still in. As long as we aren't left in the dark anymore."

"You won't be," Larchmont assured them.

One by one, the rest of the operatives agreed.

Larchmont's gaze stopped on Stephen. "I know you're our newest member. What are you thinking?"

Stephen didn't have to think long. "I'd be honored to serve alongside all of you."

Relief swept across Larchmont's face.

Then he turned toward Heidi. "And I understand that you're going to be looking for a job also."

She nodded. "I will be."

"You'll always have one here if you'd like one. As you know, we're usually based out of Michigan. But we could arrange for you to have an office wherever you're comfortable. We just opened the satellite office in DC as well. I generally split my time between Wyoming and Michigan." He glanced around the spacious ranch-style home. "This is where I come when I need to get away from it all."

"I think I could do that." Heidi squeezed Stephen's hand as if to let him know that wherever he was that was where she would be also.

Maybe this nightmare was over.

And now they would all have a new start.

~~~

Thank you for reading *Shadow Survivor*. If you enjoyed this book, please consider leaving a review.

ALSO BY CHRISTY BARRITT:

YOU ALSO MIGHT ENJOY: LANTERN BEACH BLACKOUT

LANTERN BEACH BLACKOUT

Dark Water

Colton Locke can't forget the black op that went terribly wrong. Desperate for a new start, he moves to Lantern Beach, North Carolina, and forms Blackout, a private security firm. Despite his hero status, he can't erase the mistakes he's made. For the past year, Elise Oliver hasn't been able to shake the feeling that there's more to her husband's death than she was told. When she finds a hidden box of his personal possessions, more questions—and suspicions—arise. The only person she trusts to help her is her husband's best friend, Colton Locke. Someone wants Elise dead. Is it because she knows too much?

Or is it to keep her from finding the truth? The Blackout team must uncover dark secrets hiding beneath seemingly still waters. But those very secrets might just tear the team apart.

Safe Harbor

Guilt over past mistakes haunts former Navy SEAL Dez Rodriguez. When he's asked to guard a pop star during a music festival on Lantern Beach, he's all set for what he hopes is a breezy assignment. Bree hasn't found fame to be nearly as fulfilling as she dreamed. Instead, she's more like a carefully crafted character living out a pre-scripted story. When a stalker's threats become deadly, her life—and career—are turned upside down. From the start, Bree sees her temporary bodyguard as a player, and Dez sees Bree as a spoiled rich girl. But when they're thrown together in a fight for survival, both must learn to trust. Can Dez protect Bree—and his carefully guarded heart? Or will their safe harbor ultimately become their death trap?

Ripple Effect

Griff McIntyre never expected his ex-wife and three-year-old daughter to come to Lantern Beach. After an abduction attempt, they're desperate for safety. Now Griff's not letting either of them out of his sight. Bethany knows Griff is the only one who can protect them, despite the fact that he broke her heart. But she'll do anything to keep her daughter safe—even if it means playing nicely with a man she can't stand. As peril ripples through their lives, Griff and Bethany must work together to protect their daughter. But an unseen enemy wants something from them . . . and will stop at nothing to get it. When disaster strikes, can Griff keep his family safe? Or will past mistakes bring the ultimate failure?

Rising Tide

Benjamin James knows there's a traitor within his former command. The rest of his team might even think it's him. As danger closes in, he must clear himself and stop a deadly plot by a dangerous terrorist group. All CJ Compton wanted was a new start after her career ended under suspicion. Working as the house manager for private security group Blackout seems perfect. But there's more trouble here than what she left behind. As the tide rushes in, the stakes continue to rise. If the Blackout team fails, it's not just Lantern Beach at stake—it's the whole country. Can Benjamin and CJ overcome their differences and work together to find the truth?

LANTERN BEACH BLACKOUT: THE NEW RECRUITS

Rocco

Former Navy SEAL and new Blackout recruit Rocco Foster is on a simple in and out mission. But the operation turns complicated when an unsuspecting woman wanders into the line of fire. Peyton Ellison's life mission is to sprinkle happiness on those around her. When a cupcake delivery turns into a fight for survival, she must trust her rescuer—a handsome stranger—to keep her safe. Rocco is determined to figure out why someone is targeting Peyton. First, he must keep the intriguing woman safe and earn her trust. But threats continue to pummel them as incriminating evidence emerges and pits them against each other. With time running out, the two must set aside both their growing attraction and their doubts about each other in order to work together. But the perilous facts they discover leave them wondering what exactly the truth is . . . and if the truth can be trusted.

Axel

Women are missing. Private security firm Blackout must find them before another victim disappears. Axel Hendrix likes to live on the edge. That's why being a

Navy SEAL suited him so well. But after his last mission, he cut his losses and joined Blackout instead. His team's latest case involves an undercover investigation on Lantern Beach. Olivia Rollins came to the island to escape her problems—and danger. When trouble from her past shows up in town, she impulsively blurts she's engaged to Axel, the womanizing man she's seen while waitressing. Now, she may not be the only one in danger. So could Axel. Axel knows Olivia might be his chance to find answers and that acting like her fiancé is the perfect cover for his latest assignment. But he doesn't like throwing Olivia into the middle of such a dangerous situation. Nor is he comfortable with the feelings she stirs inside him. With Olivia's life—as well as both their hearts—on the line, Axel must uncover the truth and stop an evil plan before more lives are destroyed.

Beckett

When the daughter of a federal judge is abducted, private security firm Blackout must find her. Psychologist Samantha Reynolds doesn't know why someone is targeting her. Even after a risky mission to save her, danger still lingers. She's determined to use her insights into the human mind to help decode the deadly clues being left in the wake of her rescue.

Former Navy SEAL Beckett Jones needs to figure out who's responsible for the crimes hounding Sami. He's not sure why he's so protective of the woman he rescued, but he'll do anything to keep her safe—even if it means risking his heart. As the body count rises, there's no room for error. Beckett and Sami must both tear down the careful walls they've built around themselves in order to survive. If they don't figure out who's responsible, the madman will continue his death spree . . . and one of them might be next.

Gabe

When former Navy SEAL and current Blackout operative Gabe Michaels is almost killed in a hit-and-run, the aftermath completely upends his life. He's no longer safe—and he's not the only one. Dr. Autumn Spenser came to Lantern Beach to start fresh. But while treating Gabe after his accident, she senses there's more to what happened to him than meets the eye. When she digs deeper into his past, she never expects to be drawn into a deadly dilemma. Gabe has been infatuated with the pretty doctor since the day they met. Now, can he keep her from harm? Could someone out of his league ever return his feelings or will her past hurts keep them apart? As danger continues to pummel them, Gabe and Autumn are thrown together in a quest to find answers. More important than their growing attraction, they must stay alive long enough to stop the person desperate to destroy them.

LANTERN BEACH BLACKOUT: DANGER RISING

Brandon

Physically he's protecting her. But emotionally she's never felt more exposed. The last person tech heiress Finley Cooper ever wanted to see again was Brandon Hale. Two years ago, Brandon shattered her heart. Now Finley needs protection, and, against her wishes, Brandon is assigned the job. Even worse, they must pretend to be a couple in order to find answers. Brandon, a former Navy SEAL, met Finley while on an undercover assignment in Ecuador. But he broke her trust, and now he doesn't blame Finley for hating him. As a new Blackout operative, Brandon's first assignment throws him into Finley's life 24/7. Someone wants her dead, and it's clear this person won't stop until that mission is accomplished. To keep her safe, Brandon must regain Finley's trust. Can he convince her she's more than a job to him? Or will peril permanently silence them?

Dylan

His job is to protect her. The trouble is . . . she doesn't want protection. Former Navy SEAL Dylan Granger's new assignment requires him to use both his tactical abilities and his acting skills. Hired by Katie Logan's father, his job is to protect the gutsy university professor while concealing his identity. To maintain his cover, he takes the unassuming role of her new assistant. Katie—a disgraced reporter—has stumbled upon a lead she can't ignore. Now it's clear someone is targeting her, but she refuses to back down. Her handsome new assistant is a welcome distraction from the chaos. But Dylan's skillset goes way beyond his job description, and Katie begins to suspect there's more to Dylan than he's letting on. Dylan's mission can't be disclosed—not if he wants to keep Katie safe. But as his feelings for her grow and the danger increases, keeping his secret becomes more of a challenge than he ever imagined. With innocent lives on the line, Dylan must choose between protecting Katie or savings others.

Maddox

He's on the case . . . and she's his prime suspect. Classified technology is missing, a delivery driver is dead, and former Navy SEAL Maddox King must find the culprits before a dangerous plan is enacted. To find answers, the Blackout agent must go undercover as a maintenance man at millionaire Seymore Whitlock's estate. While there, he sets his sights on Whitlock's personal assistant, Taryn Parsons, a woman who has everything to gain and nothing to lose. Six months ago, Whitlock plucked Taryn out of obscurity to become his caretaker. But with deadly incidents haunting the estate, Taryn doesn't know who she can trust—including the new maintenance man who is both intriguing . . . and unnerving. The stakes continue to escalate, and Maddox is running out of time to find answers. With the body count rising along with his list of suspects, this assignment may be his most challenging yet . . . for both his skillset and his heart.

Titus

She shattered his heart once. Can he set her betrayal aside for the sake of his country? The last person Titus Armstrong wants to join forces with is the woman who dumped him for his brother, Alex. But Presley Lennox is Blackout's best chance at infiltrating a dangerous organization known as The System and finding out more about their deadly plans. Presley Lennox wants out—of both an abusive relationship and the radical group she's become entangled with because of Alex. When Titus reappears in her life, he's like an answer to prayer—until he asks her to dive deeper into the very life she's been trying to escape. A dangerous plan is brewing that could destroy thousands of lives. Titus and Presley may be the only ones who can stop what's about to be unleashed. Failure would mean certain chaos . . . not only for them but for their nation.

ABOUT THE AUTHOR

USA Today has called Christy Barritt's books "scary, funny, passionate, and quirky."

Christy writes both mystery and romantic suspense novels that are clean with underlying messages of faith. Her books have sold more than four million copies and have won the Daphne du Maurier Award for Excellence in Suspense and Mystery, have been twice nominated for the Romantic Times Reviewers' Choice Award, and have finaled for both a Carol Award and Foreword Magazine's Book of the Year.

She is married to her Prince Charming, a man who thinks she's hilarious—but only when she's not trying to be. Christy is a self-proclaimed klutz, an avid music lover who's known for spontaneously bursting into song, and a road trip aficionado.

When she's not working or spending time with her family, she enjoys singing, playing the guitar, and exploring small, unsuspecting towns where people have no idea how accident-prone she is.

Find Christy online at:
www.christybarritt.com
www.facebook.com/christybarritt
www.twitter.com/cbarritt

Sign up for Christy's newsletter to get information on all of her latest releases here: **www.christybarritt. com/newsletter-sign-up/**

facebook.com/AuthorChristyBarritt
x.com/christybarritt
instagram.com/cebarritt

COMPLETE BOOK LIST

Squeaky Clean Mysteries
#1 Hazardous Duty
Half Witted (Squeaky Clean In Between Mysteries
Book 1, novella)
#2 Suspicious Minds
#2.5 It Came Upon a Midnight Crime (novella)
Half Truth (Squeaky Clean In Between Mysteries
Book 2, novella)
#3 Organized Grime
#4 Dirty Deeds
#5 The Scum of All Fears
#6 To Love, Honor and Perish
#7 Mucky Streak
#8 Foul Play
#9 Broom & Gloom
#10 Dust and Obey

#11 Thrill Squeaker

#11.5 Swept Away (novella)

#12 Cunning Attractions

#13 Cold Case: Clean Getaway

#14 Cold Case: Clean Sweep

#15 Cold Case: Clean Break

#16 Cleans to an End

While You Were Sweeping, A Riley Thomas Spinoff

The Sierra Files

#1 Pounced

#2 Hunted

#3 Pranced

#4 Rattled

Lantern Beach Mysteries

#1 Hidden Currents

#2 Flood Watch

#3 Storm Surge

#4 Dangerous Waters

#5 Perilous Riptide

#6 Deadly Undertow

Lantern Beach Romantic Suspense

#1 Tides of Deception

#2 Shadow of Intrigue

#3 Storm of Doubt

#4 Winds of Danger

#5 Rains of Remorse

#6 Torrents of Fear

Lantern Beach P.D.

#1 On the Lookout

#2 Attempt to Locate

#3 First Degree Murder

#4 Dead on Arrival

#5 Plan of Action

Lantern Beach Escape

Afterglow (a novelette)

Lantern Beach Blackout

#1 Dark Water

#2 Safe Harbor

#3 Ripple Effect

#4 Rising Tide

Lantern Beach Guardians

#1 Hide and Seek

#2 Shock and Awe

#3 Safe and Sound

Lantern Beach Blackout: The New Recruits

#1 Rocco

#2 Axel

#3 Beckett

#4 Gabe

Lantern Beach Mayday

#1 Run Aground

#2 Dead Reckoning

#3 Tipping Point

Lantern Beach Christmas

Silent Night

Lantern Beach Blackout: Danger Rising

#1 Brandon

#2 Dylan

#3 Maddox

#4 Titus

Beach Bound Books and Beans Mysteries

#1 Bound by Murder

#2 Bound by Disaster

#3 Bound by Mystery

#4 Bound by Trouble

#5 Bound by Mayhem

Lantern Beach Exposure

#1 Fractured Lies

#2 Shattered Whispers
#3 Unsteady Ground
#4 Troubled Graves
#5 Deceptive Shallows
#6 Secret Shores

True Crime Junkies
#1 Just the Nicest Person
#2 He Walks Among Us
#3 Never Happen to You
#4 The Dead of Night
#5 Leave the Lights On
#6 The End of the Road
#7 The Secrets She Kept
#8 Most Likely to Die

The Shadow Agency
#1 Shadow Operative
#2 Shadow Chaser
#3 Shadow Assignment
#4 Shadow Collateral
#5 Shadow Survivor

Fog Lake Suspense
#1 Edge of Peril
#2 Margin of Error
#3 Brink of Danger

#4 Line of Duty
#5 Legacy of Lies
#6 Secrets of Shame
#7 Refuge of Redemption

Vanishing Ranch
#1 Forgotten Secrets
#2 Necessary Risk
#3 Risky Ambition
#4 Deadly Intent
#5 Lethal Betrayal
#6 High Stakes Deception
#7 Fatal Vendetta
#8 Troubled Tidings
#9 Narrow Escape
#10 Desperate Rescue

Saltwater Cowboys
#1 Saltwater Cowboy
#2 Breakwater Protector
#3 Cape Corral Keeper
#4 Seagrass Secrets
#5 Driftwood Danger
#6 Unwavering Security

Beach House Mysteries
#1 The Cottage on Ghost Lane

#2 The Inn on Hanging Hill
#3 The House on Dagger Point
#4 The Bungalow on Shadow Road

The Worst Detective Ever
#1 Ready to Fumble
#2 Reign of Error
#3 Safety in Blunders
#4 Join the Flub
#5 Blooper Freak
Raven Remington Relentless
#6 Flaw Abiding Citizen
#7 Gaffe Out Loud
#8 Joke and Dagger
#9 Wreck the Halls
#10 Glitch and Famous
#11 Not on My Botch
#12 One Hit Blunder

Holly Anna Paladin Mysteries
#1 Random Acts of Murder
#2 Random Acts of Deceit
#2.5 Random Acts of Scrooge
#3 Random Acts of Malice
#4 Random Acts of Greed
#5 Random Acts of Fraud
#6 Random Acts of Outrage

#7 Random Acts of Iniquity

Cape Thomas Series
#1 Dubiosity
#2 Disillusioned
#3 Distorted

Carolina Moon Series
#1 Home Before Dark
#2 Gone By Dark
#3 Wait Until Dark
#4 Light the Dark
#5 Taken By Dark

The Sidekick's Survival Guide
#1 The Art of Eavesdropping
#2 The Perks of Meddling
#3 The Exercise of Interfering
#4 The Practice of Prying
#5 The Skill of Snooping
#6 The Craft of Being Covert

School of Hard Rocks Mysteries
#1 The Treble with Murder
#2 Crime Strikes a Chord
#3 Tone Death

Standalone Romantic Suspense
Keeping Guard
The Last Target
Race Against Time
Ricochet
Key Witness
Lifeline
High-Stakes Holiday Reunion
Desperate Measures
Hidden Agenda
Mountain Hideaway
Dark Harbor
Shadow of Suspicion
The Baby Assignment
The Cradle Conspiracy
Trained to Defend
Mountain Survival
Dangerous Mountain Rescue
Lethal Mountain Pursuit

Crime á la Mode Mysteries
#1 Dead Man's Float
#2 Milkshake Up
#3 Bomb Pop Threat
#4 Banana Split Personalities

Standalone Novels

Vacation Friends

Death of the Couch Potato's Wife

Imperfect

The Good Girl

The Wrecking

Standalone Sweet Christmas Novellas

Home to Chestnut Grove

How Her Ex Stole Christmas

The Gabby St. Claire Diaries (a Tween Mystery series)

#1 The Curtain Call Caper

#2 The Disappearing Dog Dilemma

#3 The Bungled Bike Burglaries

Nonfiction

Characters in the Kitchen

Changed: True Stories of Finding God through Christian Music (out of print)

The Novel in Me: The Beginner's Guide to Writing and Publishing a Novel (out of print)

Made in the USA
Las Vegas, NV
15 February 2025

18217803R00204